WANTED: UNDEAD OR ALIVE

/ / / /

J.R. RAIN
&
MATTHEW S. COX

ZEB CLEMENS SERIES

The Beast of Devil's Creek
Wanted: Undead or Alive

Published by
Crop Circle Books
212 Third Crater, Moon

Printed in the United States of America.

ISBN: 9798483886655

Chapter One
A Not So Quiet Afternoon

Limbo had never meant much to Zebadiah Clemens… right up until he found himself in it.

Or so he guessed. As far as he figured, mankind possessed scant knowledge of what really went on behind the scenes. If life were a theater play, the vast majority of people only saw the contents of the stage, never anything behind, beneath, or above it. His experiences thus far felt as if he'd been given a tiny peek through a gap in a metaphorical curtain at some stagehands rearranging scenery. He didn't know who he'd spotted or why they did what they did, only that they existed.

Lots of people had theories. Few had any proof, at least none they shared. People tended not to react too kindly to those sorts of ideas when they contradicted what they'd been raised to believe. For all Zeb knew or cared, *everyone* might be correct in regard to their opinions on what happened after death or the nature of the entities pulling humanity's strings.

It didn't much matter to him anymore who happened to be closest to correct. He knew for a fact 'the other side' existed, and something over there took considerable pains to keep the living in the dark.

Days like this where he spent hours idling away in the sheriff's office gave him far too much time to think about things he could neither change nor comprehend. By rights, he should have been dead a year ago... and several times thereafter. Sitting in a dusty, uncomfortably warm building only added to the discontent he felt at simply existing. Not that he minded being alive in a general sense, he rather wondered what he did to deserve his present situation.

Zeb still had yet to decide if he'd been blessed or cursed.

Perhaps the truth lay somewhere in between.

Ervin Clayton, sheriff of Silver Mesa, sat at his desk across the room from Zeb, feet up. A haze of dust motes swirled in the stagnant air between them. Deputy Jim Carberry presently struggled with one of two windows facing the street, trying to open it. Conley Meade, the youngest of the local lawmen at twenty-four, didn't seem fazed by the unusual warmth. A moan of discontent came from the holding cells down the hall. Some itinerant miner had too much to drink and gotten a bit rough with one of the ladies at Tall Kate's last night.

Being half-underground with stone walls, the holding cells tended to be a tad cooler than the front room. Zeb grumbled in his head, thinking a guy who slapped around a woman ought to be in the *least* comfortable part of the building.

"Whoever got it in their head to settle the New Mexico Territory failed to take into account the existence of the sun," muttered Zeb while fanning himself with his hat.

"That'd be someone back East, no doubt," replied Ervin. "Trick us fools out here to the desert while they stay comfy in Massachusetts."

"Massa-what-sits?" asked Clayton.

Jim turned away from the window to give the younger man a pained stare. "Boy, did you go to class at all or just farm your way to adulthood?"

"Yeah, I had schoolin'." Clayton made a show of scratching his head and acting overly confused. "Can't reckon anything about 'mass chew sets' or whatever."

Ervin, by now well aware of the new deputy's habit of being a wiseacre, simply shook his head.

After a moment of staring, Jim finally caught on that Clayton was pulling his leg and resumed fighting with the stuck window.

Zeb continued using his hat to fan himself while watching the deputy try to unstick the window. Opening it wouldn't help much unless a breeze decided to blow. Days like this made him want to find a cave somewhere and take a nap underground in the cool earth. The heat had a way of changing ordinary reality into an oppressive punishment he couldn't wait to be free of.

"Keeps on like this," said Ervin, "the Devil's gonna start sendin' souls *here* ta punish 'em."

Jim and Conley laughed.

Right as Zeb began to wonder if the pastor's stories of Hell happened to be true and he had, by some strange circumstance, ended up there, the calm of the street outside shattered to the report of gunfire. The sudden loud noise startled Jim into jumping—which finally dislodged the window.

In an instant, the attitudes of all three deputies showed clear as day on their faces. Ervin's grim expression combined the annoyance of having to attend to an unpleasant chore with his distaste for ordinary folk being hurt. Clayton's wide eyes made no secret of his eagerness to rush out there and stop the bad guys. Jim didn't show much beyond a flat look of determination as he hurried outside.

Zeb jumped to his feet. He made it to the door a half-step behind Clayton but ahead of Ervin.

Outside, townsfolk ran to the right, some ducking for cover, others sprinting. A few residents who either forgot Silver Mesa had a sheriff or simply wanted the chance to shoot someone and not get in trouble for it jogged *toward* the gunfire, weapons drawn. From the street in front of the sheriff's office, Zeb had a clear view of the fracas unfolding several doors down.

A balding man on the short and stocky side exited the bank first, two cloth bags clutched in his left hand. He fired back through the door while scooting toward the stairs leading from the porch to the street. A local businessman in a fancy suit who'd likely been on his way into the bank before the shooting started yelped in alarm while huddled in a ball on the porch, hands over his head.

The second robber to hurry outside had a long, unkempt beard and stood half a head taller than the first. Blood spray stained his filthy once-white shirt, as though he'd been standing beside someone when they took a bullet. He held two cash bags in one hand, a single in the other—no weapon drawn. Three revolvers hung from his belt.

A girl screamed, "No! Let go of me!"

Another man backpedaled out the door, dragging a black-haired young girl in a periwinkle blue dress with him as a human shield. He held her against his chest with his left arm, loot bag dangling from his fist while shooting into the bank. His gun arm passed so close to her head she could likely sight over the weapon if she hadn't flinched, averting her gaze.

Such a coating of dirt covered the men they looked as though they'd been caught outside during a dust devil. The mere sight of them struck Zeb with the odor of living in the hills for weeks without a bath.

One of the armed townies in the group ahead of the lawmen flung his gun arm up and squeezed off a pot shot at the balding man. An explosion of splinters flew from one of the porch posts beside his head, showering all three robbers and the girl with wood bits. The trio spun to face down the street, the man nearest the bank door hauling the screaming girl several inches off her feet as he tried to conceal his head behind hers.

The instant they turned, Zeb recognized her. He cursed fate for allowing a child to be part of this. Rowena Paine, the thirteen-year-old daughter of the stagecoach company man, had likely been sent to the bank by her father for one reason or another. Girls her age didn't seem likely to visit banks for fun, after all. Despite being in the midst of an abduction, the teen gawked at the man who fired at the robbers as if more afraid of him than the man kidnapping her.

All three bank robbers seemed familiar—Zeb had spent the past week or two with nothing better to do than constantly pore over the mail arriving from the Marshal's office: wanted posters. Despite Rowena's fluffy hair obscuring most of the man's face, Zeb had a fairly strong inkling he stared at Arnold "Coyote" Parrish. The other two were most likely his known associates Harry McDonald and Amos Dumont—though in the heat of the moment, he couldn't place which man belonged to which name.

At Rowena's shriek of fear, the half-dozen townies held their fire. Arnold and the balding man, alas, suffered no qualms of conscience and shot at the men—who all dove for cover behind barrels, porches, and a nearby wagon. The robber with money bags in each hand opted not to drop his loot to pull a weapon and simply ran for one of four horses standing tethered just outside the bank.

Four horses… Zeb eyed the blood spattered on the one robber. *Used to be four robbers, I reckon.*

Rowena tried to pull Arnold's arm away from her chest while also trying to whack the heels of her boots into his shins. He mostly ignored her attack, continuing to drag her to the horses while pointing his gun at the approaching group of townies and lawmen.

Zeb, not being particularly worried about getting hit, charged, intending to tackle Arnold and Rowena. Ervin and Clayton rushed after him, both doing what they could to duck and weave among the cover of porches, steps, and barrels. Jim Carberry stopped behind a waist-high barrel and raised his gun arm. In baffling defiance of the barrage of incoming fire from the bank robbers, he took his—relatively—sweet time and aimed for two whole seconds before firing once—nailing the shorter, balding robber in the chest.

Dead instantly, the man ceased shooting at the deputies and armed townsfolk; gun and money bags fell from his hands before he toppled.

Arnold pivoted to shoot at Jim, momentarily ignoring Zeb who, while closer, didn't have a gun raised. The outlaw fired twice in rapid succession, though missed in no small part due to Rowena's feverish struggling. Ervin howled in pain. His running stride fell to a stagger-step before he swerved left and collapsed behind a pair of rain barrels and a trough.

The skinny robber with moneybags in both hands stuffed his loot into a saddlebag, then drew a pair of guns and started shooting rapidly down the street at nothing in particular. Zeb ran heedlessly at Arnold. Right as he reached the gap separating the bank building from the milliner's shop next door to it, one of the armed townies leapt out and grabbed him, dragging him to safety behind the porch post. Zeb crashed to the dirt on his rear end, back against the bank wall. He had a clear view down the street toward Jim and Conley, who both dove for cover from the skinny robber's wild barrage.

Shouts of shock and dismay came from all directions, along with the shattering of glass and a few metal-on-metal ricochets. Rowena's screams took on a new tone of desperation. Rather than simply shriek, she yelled 'no' and 'let me go' repeatedly.

At that, Zeb shoved the man trying to shield him aside and lurched upright. He raced around the corner to discover Arnold had thrown Rowena over the saddle like a sack of grain and climbed up behind her. The thin man fired off the last few bullets while jumping onto his horse.

Zeb sprinted after them as they rode off, choking on the dust cloud swirling in the air in the horses' wake. Realizing he couldn't run down a pair of horses on foot and with Rowena bent over the saddle mostly out of harm's way, he skidded to a stop and yanked his gun from its holster to take aim through the hazy beige cloud at the fleeing riders. Temptation to fire only lasted an instant before he decided against it. Limited visibility made for too great a chance of hitting a bystander.

He glared at the two figures vanishing into the haze.

Rowena's screams of protest drowned under the pounding of hooves, jubilant whooping of the robbers, and the increasing din of chaos around the bank. Several more distant townspeople fired at the outlaws while a handful yelled to stop shooting due to the girl.

Son of a... Zeb scowled.

"Ervin!" called Clayton. "Sheriff!"

"I'm all right. Just a little hole," muttered Ervin.

"He's hit in the side!" yelled an unknown man. "Someone get Doc Thatch!"

"Let go of me!" shouted an alarmingly distant Rowena.

Zeb cut his gaze to one of the two remaining horses still standing unmoored by the bank railing.

Ain't like they need them no more.

Chapter Two
Wailing Ravine

Zeb spat the taste of dust out of his mouth.

The Marshal's Service wanted Arnold "Coyote" Parrish primarily for murder, but also various bank robberies as well as other episodes of larceny and assault. His bounty notice had nothing about harming women or young girls on it, so Zeb figured he'd taken Rowena in the spur of the moment as an unspoken threat against pursuit rather than some specific interest in her.

Of course, if he knew who she was, the abduction could be more than a simple case of grabbing a convenient human shield. An outlaw holding the daughter of the stagecoach manager of the area's largest city hostage had quite the advantage. Hilmer Paine would almost certainly give away any details of valuable merchandise being transported in hopes of protecting his daughter's life. Fortunately, Zeb doubted Arnold could come up with a plan like that on the fly.

The man ain't that smart, or organized, from what I understand.

Zeb spat again, adding contempt to the dirt in his mouth.

He considered it highly unlikely Arnold grabbed her on purpose. She merely happened to be in the wrong place at the wrong time. That also meant she wouldn't have any value to Arnold beyond what her presence did to ensure his getaway. As soon as he no longer needed her, he'd be just as likely to abandon her in the middle of nowhere as shoot her to keep a witness silent. Although, with his being wanted for so many different robberies and shootings already, a simple abduction wouldn't have any significant effect on any sentence he faced if caught. No matter if he killed her or let her go, he'd likely still hang. While this gave him no real incentive to kill her, it also didn't give him a reason not to.

It would take far too long to run to the stables for his horse, Jasper, or organize a search party.

Without a word to anyone or a seconds' more hesitation, Zeb jumped on a dead robber's horse and urged it up to speed. The animal didn't seem to mind having a different rider, obeying readily as if it wanted to get out of the city.

Men, at least one of whom sounded like Jim, shouted after Zeb... something about waiting and not going off alone, but he didn't pay them any mind. One thing about the unusual heat: it came with dryness. The robbers' horses kicked up one heck of a dust cloud, making it relatively easy to follow them. Arnold and his accomplice rode hard, trying to put as much distance between them and Silver Mesa as possible in as little time as they could. The horses wouldn't last long at such a pace. Given the dusty conditions, Zeb decided not to push his borrowed steed too much. Out here in the open desert of the New Mexico Territory, he could follow a the dust cloud the size of the one Arnold kicked up for several miles. Even if they pulled well ahead of him, he'd know where they went.

Of course, he didn't want to let them slip so far away he couldn't intervene if they decided to kill Rowena. Fortunately, the men had fired all their bullets in town trying to keep anyone from shooting back at them while they got on their horses. For either of them to shoot the girl, they'd have to take the time to reload at least one chamber.

Zeb paced them, keeping close enough to observe while not exhausting his horse. The skinny man periodically twisted to look back at him. He didn't attempt to reload any of his guns while riding. At the speed they pushed their horses, they'd only succeed in fumbling cartridges or percussion caps to the ground.

Rowena shifted from laying bent over the horse to sitting side-saddle in front of Arnold. For some reason Zeb couldn't see, the girl didn't attempt to jump off the horse. Either Arnold had firm hold of her or had threatened her into sitting still. She had, at least, stopped screaming and appeared to be alive.

Eventually, the robbers' horses slowed. Arnold appeared to be heading for the rougher terrain northwest of town. A low, continuous howl from the wind trapped in the nearby ravine rolled over the increasingly hilly landscape. Dirt-brown rocks, tiny bits of scrub brush, and the occasional cactus stretched out before them. Zeb hadn't spent a whole lot of time exploring this area, but knew enough about it to understand how easily someone could get themselves lost, especially if they went down into the canyon.

Go far enough from Silver Mesa, a man might even run into Natives. While he didn't doubt such an encounter could be dangerous, he also believed many stories of the Natives' viciousness to be overblown. Zeb closed in on the men cautiously, trying not to make such an amount of noise they saw him coming before he could do more than watch them kill her. If he had a rifle, he'd likely have taken a shot at Arnold, but he didn't trust using a pistol from this distance.

As if fearful of the approaching hills, Rowena began to struggle in earnest. Perhaps she hadn't been threatened as much as feared hurting herself jumping from a horse at speed. The horses' slower pace made it more tempting to try jumping clear of the saddle. A brief scuffle started with a yelp of pain from Arnold when she bit him on the arm and tried to shove herself out of his grasp. Alas, the battle ended in mere seconds with an echoing slap to the face that left her in tears.

Incensed, Zeb nudged his horse up to a full gallop.

"Hey, Ky-oat!" yelled the second man. "He's comin!"

Arnold twisted back to look at Zeb while his associate fumbled with one of his revolvers. After a second's consideration, he faced forward again and urged his animal to go faster. The tired horse begrudgingly tried to obey. The second robber abandoned his effort to reload on the run and sped up, too. Zeb ceased gaining ground on them. However he—and no doubt Arnold—knew the two horses wouldn't be able to keep this pace for long at all. While Zeb's animal had more left, it couldn't hold a full gallop for very long after the pace they'd held out of Silver Mesa.

The robbers veered away from open land, taking a treacherous path along the edge of a canyon. Though it forced them to slow to a fast walk, it had the same effect on Zeb. Rowena stopped trying to get off the horse, staring fearfully at the drop-off on the right. Barely a foot of solid ground stood between the side of the horse and a steep cliff.

"Arnold Parrish," called Zeb from about fifty feet behind them. "This is Deputy U.S. Marshal Zeb Clemens. Ain't no point in you makin' things worse on yourself. Release the girl unharmed or so help me, I will personally send you to the hereafter."

Rowena lifted her head. A curtain of thick, black hair fell away from her face, revealing a trickle of blood from her nose, stark red against her pale skin. She stared at Zeb, her eyes fearful and pleading—but also scheming. If the look she gave him said anything, she waited for a signal from him to go on the attack.

Arnold whipped his head around to glare at him briefly before facing forward and snapping the reins in a seemingly futile bid to get his horse to move faster on the narrow trail. Rocks the size of potatoes broke loose from the edge, tumbling down into the ravine below. The sharp snaps and pops of them hitting other rocks on the way down echoed up from the abyss. Sensing uneasy footing, the horse defied its master and slowed down. Arnold shouted curses, whipping at the reins harder. The animal gave a grunt of annoyance and stalled, seeming about to throw both humans off its back.

Taking the distraction as opportunity, Rowena rammed an elbow into Arnold's side and tried to jump to the left, at the solid mountainous wall away from the ravine. Arnold seized her by the throat, stalling her escape. With the manic glare of a trapped wildcat, he wrenched her back while looking around for something to do. As his horse slowed almost to a complete stop, Zeb rapidly gained ground on him, and the girl he'd taken as a hostage proved to be more of a hindrance than an insurance policy.

Seeing the murderous gleam in the man's eyes, Zeb went for his gun.

Something in the ravine appeared to catch Arnold's eye and—with one final 'go to hell' glare at Zeb—he hurled Rowena off the horse. She hit the edge of the trail for barely a second before sliding over the edge and disappearing amidst a swirl of dust into the ravine.

The loudest scream Zeb ever heard come out of a person cut off after two seconds.

Enraged, Zeb fired.

Arnold let out a yowl of pain and grabbed the left side of his head. Shouting a stream of obscenities, he swatted at his horse until it hurried forward. The second, skinny man momentarily seemed to be horrified at what his associate had done, he sat still, staring at Zeb. No sooner did Zeb pull back the hammer to take another shot, the slender bank robber yanked his head to the right, peering down into the ravine. He gaped, then chuckled.

Zeb ignored him, took aim at the back of Arnold's head. This was for throwing a little girl to her death. The son-of-a-bitch...

Both outlaws hurried along the trail. Zeb tightened his finger up on the trigger, aiming ahead of Arnold to compensate for the man's speed.

"Help!" shouted Rowena, her voice echoing from beyond the edge.

Zeb blinked, shocked to hear her still alive. He holstered his gun, scooted Jasper as far left as the animal would fit on the trail and looked down.

Rowena dangled precariously about six feet below the trail. She had a two-handed death grip on a piece of scrub brush growing out of a crack, one foot braced against a rocky protrusion… and the toe of her left shoe barely reaching a four-inch-wide ledge. The ravine wall went down at an extremely steep angle, but wasn't a flat vertical drop. At least some of her weight rested against the slope, lessening the burden on the root. It seemed Arnold noticed the root or the ledge and hoped the girl might cling to avoid a deadly fall into the ravine below. The man likely intended to force Zeb to choose between stopping to help her while he escaped, or letting the girl die to go after him. Lucky break.

"Marshal!" called Rowena. "Please hurry. My hands are slipping." The girl closed her eyes and whispered, "Don't look down" to herself a few times.

Zeb eyed the distance to the root from the trail. Even if he got down on his chest, his arm wouldn't even get close to her. *Damn, there better be a God-forsaken rope on this horse.* "Hold on, miss. Need a rope."

She gave an uneasy whimper of acknowledgment.

Ignoring the escaping robbers, Zeb hurried the two steps to his borrowed animal and tore open the facing saddlebag. Given the state of the men, they likely spent most of their days living on the land rather than around civilization. Such life habits proved unsurprising for out-laws. The more time they spent away from other people, the less likely they'd end up in prison. Amid blankets, extra shirts, a bedroll, cooking kit, and other supplies, he found a coil of thin rope likely used to secure a small tent or as a clothesline. He assumed tent because those men did not seem the type to actually wash their clothing. He hastily tied a loop at one end and secured the other end to the saddle horn.

He returned to peer over the edge. Rowena bowed her head to shield her eyes from a spray of falling dirt, dislodged by his boot. After it passed, she looked up at him. Tears, dust, and blood mixed in streams on her cheeks. The sight of a bruise from where Arnold slapped her made Zeb's blood boil all over again, but he forced himself to stay calm. Her arms trembled from fatigue. Traces of blood seeped between her white-knuckled fingers. He couldn't be sure, but the branch to which she clung appeared to have shifted, coming out of the crack an inch or so.

"Put your foot in the loop." Zeb dropped the rope over the side, trying to position the loop as close to her foot as possible.

"It's so thin," whispered Rowena.

"It's fine. Li'l thing like you don' weigh much." Zeb shook the rope once he got the loop right next to her boot. "G'won now. 'Fore that branch lets go."

Rowena appeared hesitant, but decided the cord offered her a better chance than the root. With a faint gasp of exertion, she hauled herself up enough to take the weight off her left leg. The root pulled farther out of the crack, setting loose a tiny spill of earth and pebbles. Peering down, she stuck her foot through the loop at the end.

"Other end's fixed to the horse," said Zeb in a calming tone. He dropped to one knee. "Careful now, move your hands one at a time. Slowly grab onto the rope."

As she did so, the root snapped out of the rocky crevice. Rowena shrieked, hastily grabbing onto the rope. A moment of sheer terror made her scream when one of her hands slipped, but luckily her other held fast. Gasping and whimpering, she hung on as he hauled her upward until she was close enough to grab by the wrist. With a solid grip at last, Zeb hoisted her up onto solid ground.

She collapsed into him, shuddering. Once she calmed a bit, she pulled away. Zeb noticed blood oozing between her fingers.

"Let me see," muttered Zeb, pointing to her hands.

She opened them gingerly. The root's thorns had cut into her skin, though the bleeding didn't appear serious enough for great concern. She'd likely need to go see Doc Thatch and have the wounds cleaned at least. Her dress suffered a rip or two during the struggle and fall. Arnold had slapped her hard enough to cause a nosebleed as well as a cut lip.

Looking at her state infuriated Zeb all over again, though he kept himself outwardly calm.

Any man who'd hit a girl ain't fit to walk the earth.

"What did I do?" whispered Rowena.

"Come again?" Zeb raised an eyebrow.

She exhaled hard, then winced at her cut hands. "Why did he try to kill me? He didn't have to do that."

"Nah." Zeb patted her back. "He didn't try to kill you. Saw the damn bush and reckoned you'd grab it. He wanted me to stop chasin' him, figured I'd forget him to haul you outta that damn ravine."

"Thank you," whispered Rowena, before leaning against him again, still shaking. "The other man shot Mr. Dumont. I… I think he's dead."

Zeb didn't know the bank employee too well, only that Amos Dumont, all of twenty-one-years-old, worked for Josiah Bullinger.

"And… the man who abducted me, he hit Mrs. Brennan so hard she passed out."

"Why on earth did he do that?" asked Zeb.

"He told her to hand over all her valuables, so she started yelling at him. 'Do you know who I am?' and so forth."

Well now… Zeb whistled in disbelief. As much as the idea of a man hitting a woman was beyond wrong to him, he couldn't deny a small bit of amusement at the thought of someone finally making the wealthy, arrogant socialite who spent most of her time on the porch of the Grand Mesa being judgmental about everything and everyone in her sight stop talking. Ervin once quipped it would take an act of God to make that woman stop speaking poorly of others. Turned out, it took an act of outlaw instead. Not that Zeb approved.

"Damn fool," he muttered.

"Mrs. Brennan?" whispered Rowena.

"No, the damn fool what dragged you out of town." Zeb narrowed his eyes at the distant dust trail gradually settling back to the ground, the men already out of sight. He couldn't leave Rowena to get back to Silver Mesa on her own, nor make her wait here for his return while he ran off after the bandits.

"Oh, him." She sighed. "Well, I can't be too angry at him for hitting me. I did, after all, bite him hard enough to draw blood."

"Go ahead and be angry." Zeb backed away from the edge, guiding her to the horse and giving her a boost up. "He figured dropping you would get me to stop chasin' him, but doin' a thing like this to a young'un made damn sure I ain't gonna rest until I find him."

"I'm no small child, marshal. I'll have you know I'm thirteen."

"Ahh yes, thirteen." He winked. "Almost an old maid."

She gasped, then managed a nervous laugh. She opened her mouth to say something but stopped as an eerie, echoing howl arose from the canyon below. It seemed so all-consuming and loud the entire world could hear it. Zeb, crediting the wind for the noise, paid it little mind until the girl shuddered.

"Just the wind," he said. "Nothin' ta worry about."

She swiped a strand of hair out of her eyes. "It almost sounds angry it didn't get me. Like a great, roaring demon."

"Just the wind," Zeb repeated, grasping the reins. He patted the horse affectionately before carefully guiding the animal around in a tight turn to face back down the trail.

"I know, but..." She cast a fearful glance at the canyon. "Do you think stories about this place are just stuff to scare kids or is the Wailing Ravine really cursed?"

Pondering, he began the walk back to town, leading the horse. "Well, not so long ago, I'd have said it's just stories without takin' a second to think about it. Might still be just stories. O'course, I can't say for sure now."

He gazed down into the ravine, not knowing what to make of the deep, resonant howl it gave off every so often. Someone with a strong imagination could envision the noise as the baleful cries of some gargantuan beast hiding somewhere in the maze-like canyons. Or a demon, like the girl suggested.

"Do you really think this place is cursed?" asked Rowena, sounding calm and unfazed despite her battered, disheveled appearance.

"Could be... but, I reckon' this place just got a bad air on account o' slippery-footed people walking too close to the edge." As far as Zeb knew, something on the order of twenty-six people had died to falls here over the past several years.

She cringed. "Thank you for not letting me fall."

He nodded to her.

"I'm glad it was you who came after them," said Rowena. "Sheriff would have kept chasing those men and left me hanging there."

Actually, Sheriff Ervin probably wouldn't have left town. Zeb shifted his jaw side to side. As much as he enjoyed teasing the man for his ability to ignore law-breaking when it went beyond the boundaries of Silver Mesa, he couldn't in good conscience believe the sheriff would have stood there and watched Rowena—or anyone—be carried off to an uncertain fate.

"Sheriff would've helped, but he had an unfortunate meeting with a bullet," said Zeb.

She gasped.

"Aww, he'll be all right. Just not in any shape to go gallivanting across the country any time soon."

"Oh no." She cringed. "Are you certain he's going to be all right?"

"As sure as anyone who ain't a doctor can be. Didn't look too bad."

Zeb progressively relaxed as they neared the start of the ravine. Soon, the land to his left ceased being a dangerous fall and shallowed out to a merely painful drop.

Rowena peered over at him. "Is it strange I'm not crying?"

"Nope."

"Shouldn't I be?" She bowed her head. "I almost died—plus, I watched a man get shot."

Zeb smiled up at her. "You're a strong-willed young lady. And… your heart's still going from all the excitement. Couple tears might come later on once you had a chance to quiet down and think about things. Nothin' ta worry about if ya don't. People cope with things in their own way."

She let out a hard breath, then nodded.

Zeb stared out over the desert at the distant town of Silver Mesa. They'd gone quite a bit farther than he realized, though they'd make it back in under an hour, even walking. No sense rushing at this point. For now, Arnold "Coyote" Parrish had won. However, as his former commander in the Union Army often said, 'we don't have to win every battle to win the war.'

The look on Rowena's dirt-smeared, bloody face when she had peered up out of the ravine at him burned itself into his mind. That sight would drive him onward until he found the men responsible for mistreating—and nearly killing—her.

Unlike Sheriff Ervin Clayton, his authority extended well beyond the reaches of one city, and he intended to take full advantage of that fact.

Chapter Three
The Bank

A sizable crowd had formed in the street outside the bank by the time Zeb returned to town.

Conley, the only sheriff's deputy anywhere in sight, had his hands full trying to hold everyone back from pressing into the bank building to satiate their morbid curiosity. Several women physically held onto their young sons for similar reasons. Little Heath, the son of the woman Zeb might very well be interested in, stood in front of Conley, hands up toward the crowd in the pose of a miniature deputy trying to help.

The stocky, balding bank robber still lay dead where he fell on the bank's porch, though someone had covered his face with a black hat. By some miracle, no one had taken any of the canvas sacks full of cash the dead man had been holding.

Zeb's attention went next to Josiah Bullinger, owner of the bank, who sat on the porch steps behind Conley, head in his hands as if guilty about something. The bookish fortysomething seemed a decade older than his actual years. Scraps of cloth tied around his left bicep in an improvised bandage appeared lightly blood soaked. He didn't seem too concerned about sitting beside a dead man.

Now, why's a man who's just been robbed lookin' so guilty?

"Rowena!" shouted Hilmer Paine.

The man hurried out of the crowd, away from a group of people trying to comfort him over the assumed loss of his daughter. Vera, his wife—and the girl's mother—looked up from the handkerchief she'd been sobbing into. It took her a moment to process the sight of Hilmer reaching up and helping Rowena down from the horse before she let out a scream of joy and ran over to them.

Rowena's composure finally faltered, though she smiled despite weeping as she clung to her parents. Zeb stood back and let the small family have their moment. Once it became apparent they intended to have more than a 'moment,' he let them be and approached Conley.

"Marshal," said the younger man by way of greeting. "You get 'em?"

"Not yet." Zeb set his hands on his hips, frowning. "Sumbitch tossed the girl into the Wailing Ravine. Damn near fell all the way down but for a lucky root."

"Motherless son of a…" Conley grumbled a few epithets to himself.

Zeb glanced around. "How's Ervin?"

"Jim's got him to Doc Thatch's place by now." Conley scratched the side of his head. "He'd been swearin' up a storm, so I reckon' he's gonna be okay."

"That's good." Zeb nodded once, then glanced down at the dead man. "What's he still doin' here? There're women and children about."

"Ervin wanted to wait for ol' Eli to get over here with his camera an' document it all proper like," said Conley.

Zeb chuckled to himself. "Eli Clarke, part time fancy photographer, part time pastor, part time snake oil salesman."

Conley—and a few people nearby in the crowd of spectators—chuckled. Eli arrived a few months ago from parts East. He'd opened what he called a 'portrait studio' to take pictures of anyone willing to pay for them. The man also claimed to be a pastor, though the 'miracle cures' and 'natural remedies' he attempted to sell made Zeb somewhat suspicious of his theological claims. It didn't seem likely a true man of God would be fond of swindling people. Then again, the man might genuinely believe his concoctions worked. The people of Silver Mesa generally regarded him as an eccentric oddity to be watched and/or kept at arm's length.

"What's your take on this mess?" asked Zeb.

Conley let out a breath. "Pretty simple. Four men tried to hold up the bank. Two made it out of town. Two met their maker."

"As much as I figured," said Zeb. "Four horses wait-in' outside. What happened to the first man?"

"Didn't even make it to the door."

Zeb turned around in a circle, taking in the details of the scene. The well-dressed man who had been cowering against the wall during the shooting was nowhere to be seen. Surprisingly, the porch in front of the Grand Mesa appeared empty—devoid of the high society women. An event like this would surely get them gossiping. Though, Rowena mentioned Mrs. Brennan had an altercation with Arnold. Well, more than an altercation—Arnold had hit her hard enough to knock her to the ground. Her lady friends likely attended to her wherever she'd gone off to.

He stepped past the door, surveying the inside of the bank. One roughly dressed man lay dead on his back by the counter, a shocked expression on his bald, bearded face. Blood still oozed from the bullet hole above his left eye. Another, much more well-groomed man slumped dead over the counter, arms hanging limp. A hint of gunpowder managed to sneak past the overwhelming stench of unwashed outlaw.

In the heat, the three dead men would be intolerably odorous quite soon.

Conley stepped up beside Zeb, also peering in through the door. "Sheriff wanted everything left as it was until Eli gets it on the camera thing. You know, 'case it needs to be in court. Figure since we got a camera in town, may as well use it for somethin' meaningful."

Zeb whistled. "He better hurry himself up or we'll need to burn the smell out of the building."

"Mrs. Brennan wasn't too keen on the idea of staying there on the floor, waitin' on Eli." Conley chuckled. "She didn't seem too interested in havin' her picture took neither."

"Heh."

"Reckon she'd like havin' her picture took more than most." Conley snickered. "Just maybe not with blood on her lip."

Josiah Bullinger, the bank owner, stepped into the room and sidled up next to Zeb. "Amos is dead." He gave a heavy, guilt-laden sigh. "I shouldn't have fired. Them boys wouldn't have shot anyone then."

Conley shook his head. "You don't know that, Josey."

Zeb gestured at the dead robber. "You get him?"

"Aye." Josiah nodded. "Unintentionally. Tried to shoot the other one after he raised a hand to Mrs. Brennan. Couldn't stand idle and let that kind of thing go unanswered. The four of 'em came in, guns out, demanding money. Amos and I grabbed what we could, trying to keep it all peaceful like. Then the one feller gets his eyes on Mrs. Brennan's jewelry. Orders her to hand it over. She refused. Started yellin' at him like he's some kind of help she hired who broke something."

"Good grief." Zeb pinched the bridge of his nose, slightly shaking his head. "What did she expect would happen?"

Josiah continued in an emotionless tone. "She called him an 'unwashed cretin' and told him to go away, said her jewelry was too valuable for the likes of him to touch."

Conley winced.

"Well, the cowardly bastard hauled off and punched her." Josiah gritted his teeth. "Knocked her clean out. Couldn't let that go, so I went for my gun. Shot at him, missed. Hit the other man. Except for the one who had bags in both hands, the other three started shooting back. Mostly, they tried to hit me but only managed to wing me in the arm. Poor Amos… he didn't even carry a weapon."

"Wouldn't have helped him much if he did," said Conley. "I doubt he'd have had time to reach for it."

Murmuring arose among the people outside. Curious, Zeb turned to look out the door. The crowd parted for a mid-twenties man dressed like he'd recently arrived from a downtown business district back east. His black pinstripe vest, puffy-sleeved shirt, and lavender-hued derby left him looking quite out of place. The man struggled down the street, lugging an enormous wooden box with tripod legs balanced over one shoulder and towing a wheeled cart loaded with boxes.

"Eli Clarke has arrived," said Conley in a fake-grand voice. "Make way."

The photographer stopped at the base of the porch steps and set the tripod box down on its feet before expanding the legs. That done, he gave a huff of exertion.

Zeb gave Conley a 'this should be interesting' glance. The young deputy chuckled. Heath shifted from small deputy to curious boy at the sight of the camera stuff. He, and a few other lads, crowded as close as they could get.

Josiah followed Zeb and Conley off the porch, away from the bank, so Eli could take unobstructed photographs of the scene. On the way down the stairs, the bank owner flinched, grimacing in pain.

"More than a graze, there." Zeb eyed the man's arm. The location of the red spot on the bandages suggested a bullet had gone in and stopped against the bone. "You ought'a get over to the doc."

"I suppose." Josiah looked down. "Don't seem right I'm still here and Amos isn't."

Lady luck is fickle, all right. "I know how you feel." Zeb patted the man on his other shoulder.

Eli set up the camera, then hurriedly fussed with the boxes on the cart, which appeared to contain several glass plates as well as bottles of foul-smelling chemicals that stank even worse than the robbers, enough that the curious boys kept their distance. Zeb backed up a step, unsure if even The Lady could bring him back if such substances poisoned him.

"What in tarnation is all that mess?" asked a man in the crowd.

"Portable darkroom," replied Eli in a tone some-where between stage performer and professor. "Silver nitrate, bromide salts, iodide, and other materials neces-sary to the Ambrotype process. Please give me some room to work. These materials are both expensive and volatile."

Heath zoomed over to where Zeb and Conley stood. The boy rapidly chattered on, telling them all about how he's been helping keep order.

"Seems you got this handled." Zeb ruffled the boy's wild, blond hair. "Conley, you ought to be able to keep the peace here for the time being. I got some unfinished business to attend."

Eli inserted a glass plate into the box-on-legs, then ducked under a big black cloth attached to it. He appeared to be aiming the machine at the porch.

"What's that you mean?" asked Conley. "Unfinish-ed, you say?"

"Two of them slipped away while I pulled the girl up from the ravine." Zeb narrowed his eyes. "They think they're in the clear, but the hunt is just starting."

"Need a hand with it?" Conley tilted his head.

"Nah. Town needs at least one dedicated lawman to stick around." He thought back to the strange-sounding creature he'd heard in Devil's Creek. "Reckon a couple of bank robbers won't vex me too much."

Conley started to nod but redirected his attention to a man hurrying toward them.

Zeb turned to face Hilmer Paine. Rowena and her mother had likely gone off to attend to the girl's cuts and scrapes.

"Marshall, I am in your debt." Hilmer grabbed Zeb's hand and shook it energetically. "There aren't ways known to me I can repay you for saving our daughter's life."

"Don't you worry about anything like that, now." Zeb smiled at him. "Knowin' she's home and safe is enough for me."

Hilmer let out a long, slow breath. "Do you have any ken as to why they chose her?"

"My guess is, she happened to be close enough to grab and light enough for him to carry." Zeb shook his head in contempt. "That Arnold feller don't look strong enough to hoist a grown woman around like a ragdoll."

"Sure enough." Conley chuckled. "Doubt he could've manhandled Tall Kate, even."

Zeb laughed. The local madam's name happened to be ironic. 'Tall' Kate might've even been shorter than Rowena. However, he suspected she'd likely have knocked seven shades of hell out of any man who tried to grab her as a shield during a gunfight. The meek did not brazenly operate brothels out West.

"Well now, I got some work to do." Zeb tipped his hat to the men. "Them two boys got a date with a judge, and I damn sure intend to make sure they ain't late."

Chapter Four
Powers

Zeb returned to the sheriff's office.

There, he rummaged through his desk for the wanted posters he'd stuffed in the lower left drawer. They arrived every so often from El Paso, usually several copies of each one. Ervin posted new ones on the wall in the front office as well as outside on the board. Zeb got into the habit of keeping one for himself to add to his 'reference library.'

It didn't take him long to find the ones he needed. Arnold "Coyote" Parrish had been arrested in El Paso seven months ago for another bank robbery during which two men died. Thanks to the big city having the resources for it, his notice bore a photographic likeness of the man. Though the picture was only about the size of a postcard and blurry, it had enough detail for Zeb to be confident the man who'd grabbed Rowena was, in fact, Arnold Parrish.

The $250 reward would be nice, but played little part in convincing him to go on the hunt.

Arnold's notice also mentioned known associates Wallace Warner, Harry McDonald, and Samuel Bell. This fit the evidence at the bank. Two men died, two got away. Zeb shuffled through the stack of papers for the rest of the men.

A hand-drawn sketch on another poster matched the look of the stocky, balding man who Jim Carberry shot dead on the bank porch. Wallace Warner only had a $90 bounty, suggesting only a recent foray into crime. He, too, was wanted for bank robbery though his notice didn't mention any killings.

If Jim cares to claim that one, it's all his.

He pulled that notice out of the pile. No sense keeping a dead man's face among the active bounties. Not as if he'd see the man walking around... or at least he hoped not. Three notices later, he found one with a sketch similar to the tall, slender man who'd backed out of the bank holding money bags in both hands. The notice identified him as Harry McDonald.

That left Samuel Bell, the man Josiah shot dead. Arnold's notice mentioned he had four known associates. Since Zeb had identified three of them, it left only one name to match to the dead man. Bell didn't have a notice of his own yet, or if he did, it hadn't yet made its way to Silver Mesa. It remained possible Bell died elsewhere or simply parted ways with Arnold and the poor bastard Josiah shot was his replacement, though at the moment it didn't make much difference.

He removed the notices for Arnold and Harry—the two outlaws still living—from the stack, folded them, and tucked them into his pocket. After stuffing the other papers back in the drawer, he headed down the street to the stable to get his horse Jasper. Given the unusual warmth, he took care to bring a generous supply of water.

***

Zeb retraced his steps back through the Wailing Ravine and continued past the spot where Rowena almost fell.

The two men would have been stuck following the trail around the ravine's edge for several miles until the terrain leveled off again to open scrubland. From there, they could have gone any which way. However, upon reaching the end of the canyon, tracks in the dirt led Zeb to the northwest. He doubted anyone other than the two bank robbers would've ridden through here recently enough to leave prints.

Arnold most likely believed Zeb gave up the chase to help Rowena, and thus, likely gave up pushing their horses to the breaking point. Even a man as desperate and foolish as him wouldn't drive his only means of transportation into the ground. Whether or not the men expected any pursuit to resume, Zeb couldn't say. Arnold and Harry had a significant lead, but he didn't regret bringing Rowena back to town. He couldn't have left the girl there on the trail by herself, nor could he have continued chasing the men with her accompanying him.

More than ending up shot, he worried what they'd have done to her after he 'died'—or what watching him die, then seeing him again hours later might have done to Rowena's mind if by some chance the men spared her.

Zeb scanned the horizon and the pale beige dirt surrounding him, searching for any sign of the men he hunted. Wind had already mostly erased their tracks out here away from the shelter of rocks near the ravine's end. Arnold and Harry hadn't been riding hard enough to mark the ground deeply—assuming Zeb remained going in anywhere near the same direction they took.

Darn it. Which way did they go? This thing with the Lady ought to come with some special powers ta make my life easier. He shook his head, chuckling to himself. "Somethin' tells me this ain't about makin' my life easier."

He didn't really want strange powers, nor did he even believe such things existed. Coming back from death, crazy as it was, remained something he could in theory have imagined. Except for two doctors having borne witness to it, he might have disbelieved it himself. Despite the strange twist his life had taken, he felt normal in all respects. While he could not in truth tell if hunches came from within or otherwise, he held a reasonable degree of certainty that no otherworldly powers helped him track down lawbreakers.

Nope, just me 'n only me.

The Lady, who or whatever she may be, had not chosen him to address ordinary concerns of mortals. If he were ever to exhibit abilities of a supernatural nature, they would undoubtedly be related to the extraordinary tasks she set before him.

He continued riding in the direction he happened to be going, contemplating the deeper reality of existence. Ultimately, he decided to be content with whatever happened insofar as his existence went so long as Laura and Heath remained safe to their natural ends. The utterly bizarre notion he may still be around to watch the little boy with limitless energy turn into an old man bothered him more than coming face to face with that monster in Devil's Creek.

Thus far, he'd been given no clue as to how long his 'employment' with The Lady would last. Did she intend to keep him around in excess of a normal lifespan or would he merely not die until he grew too old to track down whatever horrors she set him against? Certainly, whatever sort of being she happened to be, if she could restore his body from gunshots to the heart and brain, she could stop him from growing older if she chose to.

Upon reaching an established wagon track, Zeb put thoughts of otherworldly matters out of his mind. His knowing or not knowing all the details of his life now wouldn't change anything and served only to distract him from the matters at hand. Arnold Parrish had killed at least eight men before arriving in Silver Mesa, and outlaws though they might have been, Zeb also blamed him for the deaths of Wallace Warner and Samuel Bell. The men died during the commission of a robbery that Arnold no doubt instigated or suggested. Given the often sporadic nature of news passing across the West, he suspected Arnold to have killed more than the Marshal's Service knew about.

By his powers of observation and instinct alone, Zeb tracked the men across the New Mexico countryside for hours, pausing briefly at a small creek to let Jasper drink and rest. The oppressive heat of the day punished his water supply, so he took the opportunity to refill his canteens. Signs of recently disturbed ground here hinted that Arnold and Harry had made a similar stop some hours prior. Once Jasper appeared satisfied with enough water, and rested up, Zeb continued following his best estimation of the bandits' route for the remainder of daylight.

As darkness fell, the lawman made camp amid a cluster of boulders, where the huge stones offered a degree of shelter from the wind. Not wanting to alert the men to his presence if they happened to be close enough to see a fire, he decided on a cold camp and ate some beans straight from the can.

Even after sunset, the air remained too warm for a blanket to be comfortable, so he used it rolled up as a pillow. Gazing at the stars while waiting for sleep, he listened to the deep silence of empty land for miles in all directions, hoping to catch some faint noise indicating the robbers had not put *too* much ground between them and also camped out here.

Zeb pulled his Colt from its holster and placed it on the ground by his side, under his hand. If something woke him up, he wanted to be able to defend himself as fast as possible. Listening to silence for a few minutes eventually convinced him to close his eyes. He thought back to staring over his gunsights at Arnold and Harry riding out of the dust cloud. Generally, Zeb preferred to bring outlaws in alive to face the court system. Some deputy marshals chose to increase their odds of remaining alive by shooting first when they could and taking the lower bounty for bringing in a dead man. Arnold might have hoped Rowena caught herself and held on rather than fell to her death, but he damn sure didn't care enough about a young girl's life *not* to chance it.

If Zeb would ever be of a mind to simply shoot an outlaw rather than take him alive, it didn't come much closer than this. Any man so willing to harm a child didn't deserve to breathe. He mulled over his plan of action while trying to drift off to sleep. Walking up and shooting Arnold without a word wasn't Zeb's style, but it sure felt mighty good thinking about. No, he'd let 'the Coyote' choose his own fate. Surrender or fight.

Minutes later, the adrenaline of the day finally faded

enough for sleep to seem possible; that is, until the faint crunch of a footstep on dirt came from nearby on his left. For no particular reason, Zeb did not jump up with his gun at the ready. Instead, he merely opened his eyes all the way without moving any other part of his body. The presence approaching him did not feel threatening.

Two Native Americans walked out from behind a boulder the size of a stagecoach, both dressed simply in tunics, pants, and moccasins. One wore a headband of long beads as well as a brightly decorated vest made of similar beads. The other man's simple feather headdress marked him as a shaman of sorts. Their garb seemed ceremonial in nature. Neither carried any obvious weapons.

Both men appeared of indeterminate age somewhere between thirty and fifty.

Zeb watched them.

The Natives regarded him, their expressions giving off a sense of surprise as well as being underwhelmed. Weirdly, Zeb had an overwhelming sense they had been expecting him... and were somehow disappointed. This reeked of the supernatural. This reeked of The Lady.

Zeb suppressed his instinct to raise his gun and sat up in as nonthreatening a manner as possible.

Both Natives faded away into thin air.

Minutes passed as he stared at the empty ground where the men had been. Not a sound came from anywhere nearby.

"Well…" He exhaled. "There goes sleeping."

Chapter Five
Rawhide

In defiance of expectation, Zeb *did* manage to fall asleep after his encounter with two Native American spirits.

Prior to his experiences with The Lady, he'd have brushed the previous night's events off as a dream or hallucination and paid it no mind. Given what oddities he'd thus far seen, limited as they might have been, he decided to consider the possibility a pair of ghosts visited him. As far as he knew, living people didn't commonly make a habit of fading away where they stood.

Spirits or not, the men didn't bother saying anything to him, nor did they appear to be trying to warn him to turn around. That they didn't seem to be attempting to convey any sort of clear message meant he had little to consider in regard to the meaning of their visit.

Zeb decided to set the strange experience aside, though he couldn't fully put the men out of his mind without a mild nagging feeling he forgot to do something. He broke camp, packed everything back onto

Jasper, then checked himself over. Nothing appeared to be missing, broken, or out of place. However, a needling sense he'd missed some small detail lingered. The feeling reminded him of leaving home and not being sure if he extinguished the fireplace.

He checked over the horse as well as his person a second time, yet still had no explanation for the inexplicable notion he'd neglected to do something important. Out of desperation, he looked down to ensure he hadn't left his fly open after watering the cactus. Everything looked to be in order.

"Tarnation…" He squinted around at the landscape. "I'm forgettin' somethin' and I can't remember what it is."

Jasper nickered.

He imagined the horse thinking 'of course you can't remember it, otherwise you wouldn't have forgotten it.' With a resigned chuckle, he climbed into the saddle and resumed his trek. As best he could tell, he'd been going toward the town of Rawhide. It happened to be one of the newer settlements in the area, farther west than Silver Mesa. While he had not yet visited in person, word made it back regarding the surprising speed with which it had built up. Less than a year ago, Rawhide consisted of only a handful of homesteads. Now, it supposedly had a full downtown.

Towns out here that experienced such rapid expansion almost certainly experienced an equally rapid abandonment once the mine dried up. It seemed to be one of the unwritten rules of the West that the faster a town sprang up, the faster it crumbled. Everyone had grand dreams of making prosperous metropolises, but such big visions came with big price tags. Few mines had the fortunate longevity of the ones near Silver Mesa.

Thankfully, the city also had the luck of being a rail hub and trade center. Even if the mines there stopped giving up ore, Silver Mesa would likely remain. He couldn't say the same for places like Rawhide. Towns at the end of rail spurs had little to offer beyond what their mines produced. No ore meant no jobs, and no jobs meant everyone left to go elsewhere.

However, for the time being at least, the stories coming back to his ears spoke only of boom.

Good for them.

He considered it a reasonable assumption that Arnold and Harry headed to Rawhide with the proceeds of their recent robbery. They both struck him as the ordinary sort of outlaw fools who would flaunt their wealth while seeming unaware of the obviousness of it. Dusty, rough-and-tumble men reeking of body odor spending money like Janie Brennan and her society friends practically shouted to everyone around them that they'd robbed someone.

Perhaps there existed outlaws with at least half a brain, men who'd steal a large sum of money and lay low or get cleaned up and pretend to be from a rich family. If any such smart thieves existed, Zeb hadn't run into them. Then again, truly smart thieves didn't wave guns in bank workers' faces... they went into politics or business.

Zeb followed the signs of a moderately well-traveled route that fell short of qualifying as a dirt road. He'd gone past any point of being able to tell if the two men he tracked really came this way, though couldn't say for certain he'd seen any indication they'd veered off. The thieves had a substantial sum of money on them and would almost certainly be looking to enjoy it while they could.

This could damn well be easy. I'll find them drunk and passed out in the brothel or poker hall.

Around an hour past high noon, Rawhide came into view up ahead. The size of it initially surprised him. A downtown area of well-built wooden structures appeared comparable in scale to the business district of Silver Mesa. However, where his new home town had an 'immoral district' adjacent to the main drag as well as numerous private homes surrounding the town center, this place did not.

It looked as though a mythical giant child set up a collection of toy stores, hotels, and saloons in the middle of nowhere. Rawhide went from established downtown to bare dirt without as much as a handful of wagons to separate untamed land from civilization. Not a single private residence stood beyond half a mile of the town, save for whatever living space happened to occupy the second story above the various stores wherever the buildings had a second story. From the top of a small hill, Zeb had a view of a few distant ranch houses, some so far away they tested the limits of his vision. Rawhide built up so fast, it formed a neat grid of cross streets and evenly spaced buildings, since they did not have to expand around existing structures or property. He guessed the age gap between the oldest and newest buildings to be less than two years.

Perfect place for a man like Arnold to live it up without raising too many eyebrows.

He proceeded down the hill. Most boom towns tended to be a single street lined with a general store, a saloon or three, feed store, maybe a tiny land office, and of course, a brothel. Rawhide, however, consisted of nine streets running east to west intersected by eleven north-south streets. For a town this far west, it counted as massive—a genuine small city that popped up in an astonishingly short time span. The buildings all even *looked* new, as if they'd only been painted last month.

The eeriness of wondering what he forgot returned, making him contemplate the existence of this town as perhaps unnatural. Could he have crossed over at some point during the past several hours into some other place? Or, maybe he simply hadn't woken up yet and continued to dream.

I can't tell myself I need to stop drinking since I don't drink all that much… maybe I ought to start.

Zeb rubbed his forehead, trying to chase away the crazy nonsensical thoughts. Other than the feeble bit of doubt in the back of his mind, this town did not give off any strange energy. The people going about their business glanced at him in passing. No one appeared unusual, acted bizarre, or in any way put him on edge.

A possible explanation for the rapid buildup manifested at the end of the largest street: a rail station. Signs posted all over the building promised expansion further west would come soon while advertising the hotels, gambling, and other reasons people might choose to spend a few days here on their way to California or elsewhere. It seemed the people responsible for Rawhide existing had visions of it being a major travel stop rather than a dead-end spur—and big hopes of prosperity.

Might as well get started.

At the first stable he spotted, Zeb made arrangements for Jasper to be fed, watered, and rested. That done, he made his way around town, approaching random people, showing the two wanted notices and asking everyone who'd give him a moment of their time if they'd seen either man. The locals obligingly made conversation, seeming unbothered by his presence.

Unfortunately, no one recognized Arnold Parrish or Harry McDonald. The majority of those he spoke with seemed more enamored at being shown a printed photograph than the idea of him trying to find dangerous criminals.

That no one claimed to have seen the men potentially made sense if the thieves went straight to a saloon or brothel and stayed off the streets. Zeb noted the town had a bank, so he made that his second stop after the stable. Inside, he spent a while talking to the manger, one Richard Mooney. Fortunately for Mr. Mooney—unfortunately for Zeb—the man hadn't seen either of the robbers. Upon hearing of the events in Silver Mesa, Mr. Mooney looked into hiring a couple of men to help defend the bank for the near future.

Zeb waited patiently while a bank worker named Millie Hawthorn sketched likenesses of the two robbers from the wanted notices. The not-quite-twenty-year-old appeared to have a talent for art, as she rendered both faces in less than twenty minutes adequately enough to be recognized.

Both Zeb and Richard Mooney expected Arnold to attempt a robbery at the bank in Rawhide if, in fact, they had come to town. Zeb reasoned the two men would keep quiet until they blew through all the cash they took from Silver Mesa, then rob this bank before moving on to yet some other town, only to do it all over again. He hadn't spared the time to go asking around back in Silver Mesa if the men had done the same there, but wouldn't doubt it.

After leaving the bank, Zeb made his way from store to store, avoiding the places he thought it unlikely for men like Arnold and Harry to visit such as expensive tailors, fancy tobacconists, any place dealing in women's things… and anywhere a man might obtain a bath.

Four saloons, two hotels, three gun shops, and a gambling hall later, a random man enjoying a drink in one of the hotel bars approached Zeb in the midst of his discussing the robbery with the bartender, Frank Carney.

"Pardon there, marshal," said the mildly inebriated man, his voice unusually deep for someone so thin.

Zeb nodded at the bartender in an 'excuse me a moment' matter, then faced the stranger.

The man looked to be in his late forties with prematurely grey hair, bright blue eyes, a bushy white mustache, black silk shirt, and black pants. A stark silver pocket-watch chain draped across his vest, matching the silver bangles surrounding the crown of his hat. He could have been a wealthy railroad man trying to dress up like a cowboy, or an outlaw with money attempting to come off as respectable. Whatever his story, the man's expression held no malice.

"Can I help you, friend?" asked Zeb.

"Heard you askin' after a couple of outlaws." The man gestured at the papers. "Mind if I have a look?"

Zeb held up the wanted notices. "Look all ya like."

"Yeah, I seen that feller." The stranger gestured at Arnold's photograph. "Last night at the Lazy Weasel."

The bartender grimaced.

"Something I should know?" Zeb cut his gaze to the man behind the bar.

"Weasel's for fools and tourists," muttered Frank.

"Whole town's supposed to be for tourists," said the stranger with a bit of an eye roll.

"Ya damn well know what I mean." The bartender laughed. "Whiskey's watered down and overpriced. If you go there, you'll be robbed. Either by the establishment or the clients."

The man in black chuckled. "You mentioned this Arnold feller robbed a bank, so he wouldn't rightly care if he overpaid for anything. Gives a man a sense of being high on the hog to afford it."

"Indeed." Zeb nodded. "Mind if I ask your name?"

"Elliot Samuels."

The name rang familiar in Zeb's mind. Normally, the actual US Marshals didn't go out into the wild and enforce the law. They had deputies for that, marshal being more of a political post. Elliot, however, used to do both jobs at once—the politics part as well as the getting his hands dirty part.

"Marshal... odd finding you out here." Zeb smiled.

"Not anymore. Hung up the badge last year when I got into the railroad business. Speculation." He grinned. "Getting too old to run around after ne'er do-wells."

"Money in it, I suspect."

Elliot smiled, then gestured at the table he came from. "More than I thought possible. You look like you've been riding all day. Take a load off, have a bite."

"Much obliged. Not a bad idea."

Zeb requested a hot meal and something to drink. Relaxing for an hour or so while swapping stories with a retired marshal wouldn't get in the way of his search. No sense confronting the robbers while tired and hungry. They didn't sound to be in any hurry to skip town.

"Lazy Weasel, eh?" asked Zeb while easing himself down to sit at Elliot's table.

"Yep. I mostly avoid the place myself. However, I couldn't turn down an invitation to a high stakes bit of poker last night."

Zeb whistled. "How did it go?"

"Came out ahead." Elliot laughed. "Not by a whole lot, mind you, but it beats losing my pants." He pointed at Zeb. "Which is a distinct possibility in that place. Keep your eyes open."

"Will do." Zeb leaned back, drinking down most of his water in one breath.

"Get this man some more water," called Elliot.

Frank waved Zeb over to collect his dinner, which he'd fetched from the kitchen behind the bar. The hotel looked a bit too fancy of a place for him to take a room here, but the food smelled good—better than he usually had back home.

May as well let the day get longer. Might make Arnold drunker—and easier to take in.

Or not.

Chapter Six
The Lazy Weasel

Following a pleasant meal and conversation with the retired marshal, Zeb set out to explore Rawhide in search of the Lazy Weasel.

Despite the approaching twilight, a surprising amount of people still walked the streets. The majority appeared to be out-of-towners likely there for a day or two while waiting on a train or coach to take them to their ultimate destination. They didn't appear as well-to-do as the people who frequented the downtown area of Silver Mesa, nor did they have the permanent grunge of miners and prospectors. He figured them mostly settlers or homesteaders in search of a plot of land to set down some roots, much the same as he had in mind when he originally headed out west.

The Lazy Weasel stood at the northernmost end of the second north-south street from the west edge of town, putting it more or less at the outside corner. To its left stood a small, terribly austere hotel. To its right, a feed shop. Behind it lay open scrubland and a pair of outhouses. The oddity of a small city abruptly shifting to untamed ground caused him to stare. He'd seen small mining communities built in the same manner, but they only consisted of four to six buildings. Rawhide's sheer size made it unusual not to have at least a few more widely spaced properties away from the downtown.

It really did look like this town simply appeared overnight out of thin air, as if transplanted from somewhere else. Still, he didn't feel anything unearthly in the air—a visit from Native spirits notwithstanding—so shrugged it off as nothing more sinister than some wealthy people spending a whole lot of money to build a town fast in hopes of becoming even richer by taking advantage of people's desire to travel west.

A carved bas-relief of a sleeping weasel hung on the wall above the front door—or at least the best attempt of a woodcarver who had never laid eyes on a weasel. Zeb couldn't claim to have seen one either, though had a feeling they didn't look like the little creature before him. Good chance weasels weren't the size of dogs with big, goofy crossed eyes.

Poor critter looks like a beaver that done annoyed a bear.

Being so new, the saloon didn't give off any detectable sense of class. It didn't look like a dive, nor did it seem ritzy. A low din of people talking inside came through the wall, punctuated by the occasional laugh or whoop of gambling victory.

Shaking his head at the pitiful fake weasel, Zeb went inside.

A haze of tobacco smoke hung near the ceiling. The air tasted of mid-grade whiskey, cigars, and new wood. Among roughly twenty tables scattered about the room sat upward of fifty men, most of whom engaged in card games or dice. The bartender, a late-thirties man with slick black hair and a thin mustache, regarded Zeb with a casual glance.

The lawman scanned the faces of the patrons, sweeping his gaze across the room. One by one, the men seemed to sense the presence of a man searching for someone specific. They stopped gambling to stare back at him. Gradually, the room fell silent. Arnold did not appear to be present—however, he spotted Harry McDonald at the back of the room sitting at a table adjacent to an unattended piano with three other men, one of whom was so big he made the rest look like adolescent boys. He barely fit in the chair, likely six and a half feet in height with shoulders half again as wide as anyone else in the room. Zeb couldn't help but notice the big man's Union Army uniform shirt. It appeared battle-damaged and likely genuine. Considering it fit a man so large, it had to have been made for him and not simply taken as a souvenir.

Zeb paused, staring at the huge guy gambling with the man he'd come here to arrest.

That fella's gonna be a problem.

One did not wear Union regalia around here unless they itched for a fight. While neither the Confederacy nor the Union enjoyed a major presence in the New Mexico Territory, the citizens tended to belong to one of two camps. Either they wished to put it all behind them and didn't take kindly to any reminders of the recent strife, or they happened to be from the former Confederacy, having moved west to escape the destruction as well as any perceived 'oppression' from the north.

Given the size of the man, he might have continued wearing the uniform shirt purely because he didn't have anything else big enough. Or, perhaps, he *wanted* to set off a brawl. Worse, a collection of twenty or more glasses in front of the huge man implied he'd been drinking heavily. While a man of his size *would* need quite a bit of whiskey to become drunk, it sure looked as though he'd had enough.

The bank robber froze where he sat, staring at Zeb like a cornered jackrabbit. On the tall side, slender, with bushy, unkempt hair—and still wearing the same blood spattered shirt—the man's face more or less matched the drawing on the wanted notice. He'd evidently been so enamored with their profitable heist he'd gone straight to drinking and gambling rather than clean himself up.

"Harry McDonald," said Zeb, approaching him. "Need ta have a word."

The man twitched. He seemed as likely to go for a gun as he did to leap over the piano and run for the back door. Zeb dropped his hand closer to his weapon and took a few steps toward the table, ready to draw or give chase.

A look of inspiration dawned in Harry's eye. He clapped the big Union soldier on the shoulder and hastily whispered something into his ear. For a few seconds, the drunk man appeared confused until Harry pointed at Zeb. The instant the former soldier noticed the US Marshal's badge, he went from dazed calm to red-faced.

Roaring, the big man leapt to his feet, throwing the table to the floor under a fluttering storm of playing cards, empty glasses, and money. He spun to face Zeb, head nearly touching the ceiling, arms raised to either side in a stance as if he couldn't decide if he wanted to punch or simply break Zeb in half.

Uh oh.

"Y'ain't draggin me back!" bellowed the soldier.

"Whoa. Hold on now." Zeb raised a hand. "I'm not

—"

Enraged, the soldier let loose another mangled war scream and bum-rushed him.

Zeb threw himself to the side like a matador, barely avoiding a fist almost as big as his entire head. Surprisingly fast for his size, the man whirled around and caught him in the chest with a backhanded left swing that catapulted him off his feet. In a seeming instant, Zeb found himself on his back atop a table, wheezing for air. The three men sitting around him scrambled out of their seats as the giant soldier stomped over.

"Listen," rasped Zeb. "I ain't—"

The soldier continued roaring incomprehensibly as he grabbed two fistfuls of Zeb's shirt and hauled him into the air. He didn't much appreciate being thrown around like a child, but the huge guy appeared well beyond reason at the moment. As the saloon blurred into a spin around him, Zeb hammered his fist into the man's face a few times, though the punches seemed to have little effect on the enraged drunk.

Cutting loose another howl of rage, the man hoisted him higher, then hurled him straight down on the floor. Zeb crashed into the floorboards so hard he bounced. Stunned from having all the wind knocked out of him, he barely put up a defense as the Union soldier grabbed him by the back of the neck and his belt, hauling him into the air like a battering ram, aiming to plow him headfirst into the bar.

Zeb flung his arms forward, shielding his face enough to avoid being knocked senseless as he collided with the bar.

"I ain't goin' back there!" bellowed the man before yanking Zeb away from the bar and throwing him upright into a backpedaling stagger, then cocking his arm back for a punch.

Arms flailing for balance, Zeb leaned away enough for the man's overextended haymaker to miss by an inch. Coarse arm hair grazed his nose and cheek. The lack of contact on such a heavy punch sent the drunken man lurching over the bar. Zeb took the opportunity to retaliate, pouncing on the man and hammering his fist into the soldier's head twice. Alas, the attack proved ineffective. He may as well have been trying to clobber a sack of horse feed. Zeb took a step back and shrugged at the room as if to say 'what am I supposed to do here?'

As the soldier shoved himself upright, a glint of glass caught Zeb's attention: a mostly empty bottle rolling across the bar on its way to the floor. He lunged toward the bar, grabbing the bottle before it fell over the edge. The instant the angry drunk spun to grab him, Zeb clubbed the huge man over the head. The bottle bounced off the soldier's skull with a hollow *clank*. The giant's eyes rolled halfway up into his head. He momentarily stood frozen in place. Zeb eyed the bottle, impressed that it hadn't shattered. He considered whacking the soldier with it a second time, but before he could decide what to do, the man collapsed straight down into a heap.

Zeb grunted, set the bottle on the bar, and looked behind him at the now upside down table near the piano. Sure enough, Harry had slipped away during the commotion.

"Damn," muttered Zeb. He glanced at the bartender while indicating the mostly unconscious soldier. "What's his story?"

"Ehh…" The bartender shifted uneasily. "Willie here's not exactly discharged in good standing."

"Deserter." Zeb grumbled. The man likely had a small bounty on him, doubtfully enough to be worth the hassle of attempting to arrest someone so large and strong. Besides, he had more pressing issues to attend. "When he wakes up, tell him I ain't here for him." He walked across the room to where his hat landed, retrieved it, and put it on. "Now, if you'll excuse me…"

Chapter Seven
Stings

Zeb ran out the back door of the Lazy Weasel Saloon.

A quick glance straight ahead past the two lonely outhouses made it fairly obvious Harry hadn't gone that way: vast open scrubland offered nowhere to hide. He jogged to the left, following a narrow alley back to the street in front of the place. When he emerged on the first crossing street, he skidded to a stop and did a full turn. None of the small fences, barrels, boxes, or other stuff lying around showed signs of being recently disturbed.

If Harry had come running through here in a panic, maybe someone he bumped into would still be yelling at him. Alas, no obvious signs of a fleeing outlaw greeted him.

Rawhide is large for a boom town, but still too small for an outlaw to hide in. He's going to skedaddle.

Trusting his instinct, Zeb jogged down the street looking for a stable. The town had three of them. One advertised horses for sale while the other two only rented stalls on a temporary basis, essentially being 'horse hotels' for travelers. He proceeded to the nearest one at a light run, earning curious looks from passersby.

He jumped the fence surrounding the yard in front of the stable building, attracting the attention of three adolescent boys who'd been sitting on the porch. He waved at the kids to stay back and barreled across the yard to the barn door. Alas, the curious trio ignored his directions and followed.

The rattling of saddle straps and nervous muttering inside the barn set off a burst of mixed emotion. He'd likely found Harry… but did not want to set off an exchange of gunfire while having three young boys so close behind him. Zeb had no time to yell at the kids for getting in the way, nor could he stop inside the doorway, gun pointed, and demand Harry surrender. If the bank robber proved foolish enough to go for his gun even though Zeb had the drop on him, a hasty shot could easily go stray and catch one of the boys.

So, he did the only thing that seemed reasonable in the moment—charged.

Likely hoping to avoid notice, Harry McDonald had crammed himself into the stall beside the horse, trying to get the saddle on its back before leading it out. He turned at the thudding of Zeb's boots on the floor, gave a scream of alarm, and—sure enough—grabbed one of the three guns on his belt.

Three small gasps behind him announced the boys saw the gun. He couldn't tell if they reacted with fear or excitement purely from the sounds they made, and didn't spare the second to look back to see if they'd taken cover. Harry sidestepped out of the stall, not fully raising his gun in time before Zeb got close enough to swing.

As Zeb's fist crashed into his jaw, Harry fired a shot

into the floor beneath his horse, causing the animal to rear in panic. The skinny man reeled backward, arms and legs flopping around like a limp marionette. He lacked Willie the Union Deserter's ability to shrug off punches, ending up loopy and disoriented from only one hit.

Zeb grabbed Harry's forearm and smacked his hand into the nearest stall door until the black Colt revolver fell from his grasp with a heavy *thud*. Harry drove a left-handed punch into Zeb's gut; though painful, it didn't have enough *oomph* to do much more than cause a discomfited grunt. Zeb throttled the man around the neck, banging his head into the wall several times.

"Where's your buddy? Where'd Arnold go?"

Harry grabbed Zeb's wrists, trying to dislodge his chokehold.

"You gonna kill him?" asked one of the boys.

Zeb shifted his gaze to the stable door. Three small heads poked around the left side of the doorjamb, staring at him. The youngest, likely around eight or so, was closest to the floor. The middle boy stooped over him with the eldest, no older than eleven, up on tiptoes so it appeared their heads had been stacked atop each other. Resemblance in their faces made it obvious they were brothers.

"Trying real hard not to," said Zeb.

"What did he do?" asked the middle boy.

"I ain't did nothin!" shouted Harry. "You boys get over here and help get this killer off me!"

Zeb bonked Harry's head into the wall again. "Bank robbery. Murder. Kidnapping."

The kids went wide-eyed.

"You a lawman, mister?" asked the oldest.

"I am." Zeb looked back at Harry. "Deputy U.S.

Marshal, in fact."

Harry grabbed for one of the guns still hanging on his belt. Zeb flung him to the floor, stepped on his neck, and disarmed him, tossing the revolvers across the floor out of reach. Harry rolled, wrapped himself around Zeb's left leg, and bit him on the shin. Zeb reflexively slugged the man in the head, this time knocking him out.

"Well, I'll be damned," muttered Zeb. "Seen desperate men do desperate things before, but behavin' like a half-blind cougar ain't one of them."

The boys laughed nervously.

A few seconds later, Harry groaned and pushed himself somewhat up off the floor.

"I see you are still with us." Zeb pulled the man upright. "You gonna be cooperative and such? Judge'll likely go easier on ya. Might even avoid hangin'. You look like the type of man who'd much prefer to be alive in jail than danglin' by the neck. Where's Arnold?"

"Dunno," said Harry. "We split up. He could be anywhere."

The man's tone didn't sit right. Zeb rested a hand on Harry's shoulder in an almost gesture of camaraderie. He smiled briefly, then shoved him face-first into the wall, splitting his lip open and almost breaking the man's nose.

"Let me ask again. Where'd Arnold go?"

"No damn idea." Harry gestured at the boys. "See? He ain't no marshal. Hittin' me like that."

"No worse than what you and your buddy did to that little girl. In fact, her lip bled more than yours is now. Let me correct that oversight." Zeb gripped him by the shirt collar, and drew him backward, about to introduce his face to the wall again.

"Wait!" Harry thrust his hands forward, trying to

catch himself. "All right. He's headed to Harlon's Pass. Said he knows someone there. Place he can lay low. Told me to go somewhere else an' forget I knew him for a time."

"Harlon's Pass," said Zeb in a pondering tone, weighing how much to believe what he heard.

Beating information out of outlaws didn't usually work. Men had a tendency to say whatever they could think of to make the beating stop. However, this guy seemed to have a genuinely low pain threshold. A physical fight between them had about as much chance going in Harry's favor as Zeb besting Willie the Deserter without using a weapon.

Scrawny, underfed, cowardly…

"Yeah. Swear." Harry waved his hands back and forth. "Said that's where he's goin'. Crazy, though. He ain't never mentioned the place before. Like he got the idea out the blue or somethin'. You best hurry an' get over there afore he changes his mind."

"I'll do that." Zeb dragged him toward the door. "Right after I drop you in a cell."

Harry yowled in desperation as he twisted away from him and made to sprint away. He nearly made it out the stall door before the middle boy stuck his bare foot out and tripped him. Harry slipped in the hay scattered across the floorboards and crashed into a heap in the dirt outside the stable.

Zeb shook his head. "This just ain't your day, McDonald."

"He's got a gun!" yelled the smallest boys.

Harry whipped his arm up, holding a tiny silver Derringer. Zeb lunged at him. The little pistol went off with more of a *snap* than a bang. Furious and exasperated, Zeb didn't hold back, hammering his fist into the scrawny outlaw's jaw with all his strength. A soft crunch accompanied the man's jaw breaking. The former bank robber slumped unconscious to the floor, blood and one tooth dribbling from his mouth.

Zeb glanced at boys, who congregated by the wall next to the door. All three seemed quite excited at the goings on. None looked hurt.

"You boys all right?"

They nodded simultaneously.

Zeb smiled at the middle boy. "Quick thinkin', lad. Appreciate it."

The child beamed.

An inaudible sigh slipped from Zeb's mouth as he glanced around. *Now where in the heck did that bullet go?*

Within seconds, a stinging pain in his left thigh provided the answer. Zeb looked down at himself. A small red spot had appeared on his pants with a tiny hole at the center. Over the next few seconds, it began to hurt like a red-hot knitting needle stabbed into his muscle. He clenched his jaw tight.

How funny is that? Gettin' killed don't hurt near as much as this damn pea-shooter.

Chapter Eight
Damned

A hot bath gave Zeb a chance to think about his next move.

It also offered him the opportunity to wash blood and road dirt off, as well as made for a convenient excuse to rest for a while. Willie the Deserter had battered him a bit more than he felt at the time. The beating caught up to him during the process of taking Harry to the local jail. The Rawhide sheriff proved remarkably amenable to assisting the Marshal's Service upon seeing the wanted notice for Harry. They'd hold him here until a telegraph came back with confirmation. By now, he expected Sheriff Ervin or at least Deputy Jim Carberry had sent word to El Paso for him regarding the bank robbery. If not them, then definitely bank owner, Josiah Bullinger, had reported the robbery.

Harry McDonald would spend a couple days in the Rawhide jail before they packed him on a train under escort to El Paso where other marshals would take over. Zeb's part of apprehending him should be over. The deputy marshal would have fully committed himself to resting if not for the need to find one more bank robber.

The gunshot in his leg changed from stinging pain to a dull ache to an itch. After half an hour soaking in hot water, the itching became burning again. Zeb still couldn't quite get used to seeing unexplainable things like the hole in his leg disappearing mere minutes after he'd been shot. A mark similar to a nasty insect bite remained on the spot, though it no longer bled. When the itching grew inexplicably worse, he poked at the spot— and felt a small lump under the skin.

Damn bullet's still in there.

He shifted his jaw side to side, weighing the idea of cutting himself open to get rid of it. Couldn't hurt any worse than the bullet going in. Unfortunately, his knife remained on his belt, which presently sat out of arm's reach on the small bench a short distance from the tub. The hotel had two bathrooms available for rent. He'd had to wait for water to be heated and brought inside by the bucket load. The tub's drain connected to a pipe that simply ran out the wall to dump the water on the ground behind the building.

Bunch o' work to fill, easy to empty.

Zeb's idle scratching of the wound stopped when his finger brushed a protrusion that hadn't existed a moment earlier. He looked back at his leg to find a pea-sized red mass having grown out from the spot. Alarmed, he stared in bewildered horror as the orb of skin darkened to purple, then split open. Through a dribble of blood, a tiny bullet 'hatched' from its enclosure before falling into the tub. Amid a sudden, intense itching, the deflated skin bubble shrank and sealed to resemble a scabbed-over puncture wound.

Zeb rubbed the spot. A pronounced soreness beneath

the skin suggested the damage the bullet caused on the way in remained at least in part. It seemed whatever unnatural knack he had for not dying decided to leave him a small reminder to avoid being shot whenever possible.

"Makes no damn sense," whispered Zeb to himself while picking at his chest.

The bullet responsible for killing him a few weeks ago when Silas shot him hadn't even left a mark. It didn't hurt at all. One moment, he'd been standing there being shot at by the Diamonds Gang. The next, he lay on the ground beside corpses. He found it irritating that a superficial wound hurt significantly more than a fatal one.

"S'pose that's how it goes. It's the little things that cause the most consternation."

He reached down between his knees, feeling around the bottom of the tub until he located the bullet. Once he found it, he held it up, pinched between two fingers of his soapy, dripping hand. He'd thought of it as pea-sized, but it appeared visibly smaller even than that. Though he'd been shot multiple times before, he had not yet looked directly at a bullet after it had been inside his body.

Zeb rolled it back and forth between his fingertips, marveling at the circumstances responsible for his being able to shrug off a gunshot wound. He'd seen too much at this point to continue to doubt reality as a crazy dream. The only reasonable choice he had left would be to embrace it for as long as it lasted. Not that he required any fear of final death to do so, but he figured the more good he could do for people thanks to this craziness, the longer it might last. Ironically, being unable to stay dead made him happier to be alive.

This was inside my leg. Zeb carefully set the bullet on the tub edge, intending to keep it as a souvenir. He entertained a brief daydream of being an old man sitting at a table with several large jars full of bullets he'd absorbed over decades or even centuries. Again he glanced at the tiny bullet and chuckled at the oddity of it leaving his body.

Well, I'll be damned.

He laughed to himself.

"Then again, maybe I am."

Chapter Nine
Harlon's Pass

The following morning, Zeb met with the Rawhide sheriff, an older man with the mildly humorous name Dusty Cobb.

He had to be near sixty years of age, likely given the post of sheriff as a political favor to whoever bankrolled the town. Despite the possibly suspicious nature of his appointment, he treated the Harry McDonald situation on the level.

Zeb sent a telegraph to inform the Marshals Service that he'd arrested Harry to forestall anyone else trying to poach the bounty payment. Confident the local lawmen would do the right thing, he took a quick breakfast before collecting Jasper from the stables and riding out of town in the direction of Harlon's Pass.

Both Sheriff Cobb as well as the stableman gave him the same directions. He'd never been to Harlon's Pass before, though had heard it mentioned. Going there sent him further west and a little bit south, about as opposite as possible to the direction of his home in Silver Mesa.

Harry had perhaps believed Rawhide would be safer due to it being closer to civilization—but not *too* close. Outlaws generally went west when spooked. Many had the belief that going eastward put them in closer proximity to 'civilization' and the oppressive laws they disliked. They varied from literal outlaws to men who simply rejected the idea any government—or lawman— had the right to tell them what to do. A certain element much preferred the ability to take matters into their own hands, resolving any dispute with a brief gunfight rather than a lengthy courtroom argument.

Zeb didn't much care about the notion of forcing civilized law over the land. He primarily wanted to help protect people who couldn't defend themselves from men like Arnold Parrish and the Diamonds Gang. As far as he knew thus far, Arnold had nothing to do with the Diamonds. In fact, the gang appeared to be keeping their distance from Silver Mesa ever since he wiped out their camp. Surely, some manner of crazy stories circulated among the members of the gang about him. One marshal walking into an entire camp of Diamonds and killing them all, save one man who managed to run away? A story like that would either be terrifying or laughable.

If it keeps them out of Silver Mesa, let 'em tell stories.

From what Sheriff Cobb told him of Harlon's Pass, it happened to be a rather small town surrounded by ranches. Not being connected in any way to mining kept it small and isolated but also offered some degree of protection against sudden abandonment. People went to Harlon's Pass because they wanted to live there, not chasing the fortune of silver or gold. They wouldn't leave the area because their hopes of riches evaporated. A place like that ought to be quiet, ought not to have much to attract the attention of men like Arnold Parrish.

Perhaps the smartest thing the fool's done. No one would think to look for him there.

Zeb rode until nightfall. He made camp, had a meal of hard tack and canteen water, and settled down for sleep. Part of him expected a visit from Native spirits, but none showed themselves. He knew the Navajo lived somewhere in this area, though couldn't imagine a town like Harlon's Pass would have been built in a place liable to suffer frequent attacks. He half smiled to himself at the thought of how he'd handle an unprovoked attack. Natives seeing him die then coming back would probably end up worshiping him as some sort of powerful spirit.

In a sense, he could understand their anger. To them, he was a foreign invader, even though he'd known no other land. He'd heard all manner of stories concerning savage attacks against settlers, including women and children. Some were likely true, but how many times had the US Cavalry gone in and massacred the Natives? Seemed no one side had the moral high ground. The last thing he wanted to do was make any of it worse.

Best thing for everyone involved if I don't cross their path.

***

Two days after leaving Rawhide, Zeb arrived at Harlon's Pass.

He rode Jasper down a meandering dirt path on the side of a scrub-speckled hill. Struggling swaths of almost-green attempted to grow on the sunbaked dirt. Ahead and below, the land spread out in a myriad of colors from browns to green where human hands irrigated the soil. The town of Harlon's Pass sat a short distance from the opening of a canyon and looked much like he expected a small pop-up frontier town to look. Seven buildings clustered together along a single dirt street, with a church a distance off to the west.

Ranch homes and farms surrounded the downtown area, the closest looking to be about a mile away. Others dotted the landscape, with the farthest one in sight likely half a day's walk away from downtown.

Roughly two hours past noon, Zeb reached the point where the hint of a wagon trail he'd been following met the street running through the center of the tiny downtown. He happened upon a funeral procession making its way from the church. Not wanting to be rude or interfere, he stopped well short to give the people room to go by, and removed his hat. Some of the mourners glanced at him in much the same way people tended to glance at strangers. None gave off any particularly strong reaction to his presence.

An older teenage boy broke away from the procession and approached him. He seemed about seventeen or so, fairly robust, and apparently used to farm work.

"Afternoon, sir," said the boy with a curt nod.

"Howdy."

The boy glanced at the funeral. "You a relative of Ollie?"

"I am not. Here on business." Zeb patted his badge.

"Oh. Uhh, marshal." The boy offered a handshake. "Welcome to Harlon's Pass. I'm Everett."

"Zeb Clemens." He shook the lad's hand, finding the boy's grip as strong as expected.

"Your business have to do with Ollie?"

"No. Should I be concerned?"

Everett edged closer, lowering his voice. "Ollie used

ta work for my pa. We found him dead out in the field the other day. Pa thinks he got trampled by a horse or somethin' but rumors going around it weren't nothin' natural what did it."

"Nothing natural?" Zeb let a long, slow exhale slide out his nostrils while keeping a straight face.

Common folk often came up with wild stories to explain things they couldn't otherwise understand. However, he no longer immediately dismissed such things as flights of fancy, especially considering Harry told him Arnold Parrish made the decision to go here seemingly out of nowhere. He might be assuming too much, but 'outside forces' could have influenced the bank robber as a means to bring Zeb here.

"That's what they're sayin', marshal." Everett nodded toward the funeral procession. "Ollie's head, well… you ever see a plow horse step on a pumpkin?"

Zeb cringed. "Can't say I have, but the mind paints a picture I'd just as soon *not* bear witness to. Seems a sort of thing a horse could do to a man."

"It does." Everett set his hands on his hips, nodding. "Crazy talk, if you ask me. Just a wild horse out of control." He fidgeted. "Beast what did it must'a run off. No one rightly saw it."

"How come people are telling stories about it then?"

"I don't rightly know, but they are." The boy sighed wistfully, almost chuckling. "Speaking of stories, my little sister Ada's got an imagination. Girl's been telling people she's seen a monster outside at night."

Zeb smiled. "People around here so on edge they take a little girl's story to heart?"

"Well, a fella named Mr. Brooks thought he'd seen something crazy, too. He's a lot older than nine." Everett scratched his head. "Dunno if he saw the same thing as my sister, but hearin' a grown man kinda agree with what Ada said set the old ladies talking."

"As they so often do." Zeb tried not to laugh out loud in earshot of a funeral. "Ollie had a lot of family?"

"Nawp." Everett shook his head. "No one what lived here. Everyone knows everyone here, so I guess you could say we're all his family in a way."

"Aye." Zeb watched the procession of mourners head away from the downtown, then pointed to his left. "Where are they going? The church is that way."

"Graveyard ain't near the church. Pastor thought it might unsettle people havin' it too close to that end o' town after what they found in the canyon."

Zeb arched an eyebrow. "What did they find in the canyon?"

"Indian stuff. Reckon it's a burial mound or somethin'." Everett scrunched up his nose. "I ain't never been out there, but they said the place felt wrong, ungodly. Evil in the air. Don't rightly know their ways. Whatever it is, it spooked the pastor and the elders. They wanted to put the dead as far from the canyon as they could."

The strange sense that Zeb had forgotten something returned. He still couldn't place any exact cause for the feeling, but Harlon's Pass began to unsettle him. The longer he sat there looking at the black-clad people in the funeral procession march past the small collection of buildings, the more he felt the need to do *something*. What, exactly, he didn't know.

"So, what brings you here?" asked Everett, peering up, squinting at the sun behind him.

Zeb set aside his unexplained sense of urgency and fished out the wanted notice for Arnold Parrish, which he unfolded and held up so the boy could read it. "I have a reasonable suspicion this man might be hiding out in town."

Everett reached for the paper. "May I?"

Having no reason to suspect the boy would damage the paper, Zeb let him take it.

"Hmm." Everett held the photograph close, studying it for a moment before handing it back. "He does look kinda familiar. Might have seen him a day or two ago over at Branch's."

Zeb raised an eyebrow. "Branch?"

The boy pointed at the downtown. "General store. Man what runs it is Eugene Branch. He's kinda like our mayor, too."

When Zeb looked to his right, he couldn't help but notice the funeral procession walk by a Native American in a shaman's regalia standing out in the open about twenty paces from the last building in the 'downtown'. Though the mourners passed so close they could've grabbed him, not one man, woman, or child reacted to the Native's presence. Considering what Everett said about the town being so spooked at the mere discovery of abandoned Native artifacts they relocated the cemetery, it struck him as incredibly strange for the people to be so calm.

Or maybe they can't see him.

When the shaman turned his head to look at Zeb, it hit him. He was one of the same two spirits who'd appeared at his campsite days ago. This time, the man's demeanor did not give a sense of disappointment. If Zeb were to put words to the man's expression, they'd be something like 'well, you're here. Get on with it.'

"Alright, alright," muttered Zeb. "Once I take care of Arnold."

"Pardon, marshal?" asked Everett. "Didn't quite catch that."

"Nothin' you need worry about, son." Zeb smiled. "Just an old man talking to himself."

"You don't look old."

"Heh. Thank ya."

Everett gestured at the wanted notice. "Bank robbery? Ain't no bank here. Why's a man like that bother with a town like ours?"

"Don't rightly know. Reckon he's just looking for a quiet place to hide out until he thinks we've stopped hunting him." Zeb peeled his gaze away from the spirit to look at the boy. "Appreciate it if you let a couple men around town know there could be an outlaw in the area. Try not to make too much of it. Don't want him getting wind of me bein' here and decidin' to slip away in the night."

"Of course." Everett nodded. "Be glad to help. Well, I ought'a get on with the funeral afore they stick Ollie in the ground."

Zeb nodded.

The boy waved farewell and ran off to catch up to the funeral procession. Zeb watched the people march until they vanished from sight beyond a distant hill.

Soon, only the shaman remained staring at him.

He sat there on Jasper's back looking at the spirit, trying to figure out if The Lady had anything to do with this or if different spirits sensed whatever he'd become. Perhaps he could see the dead since he'd been to their world several times and come back. The mood wafting from the ghost did not seem hostile. If anything, he looked impatient and a touch worried, fixing Zeb with an expectant stare. After a few minutes, the haunt faded away. It couldn't be a coincidence some little girl saw a monster that a grown man also caught a glimpse of in the same place Native spirits popped in to make urgent faces at him.

Damn. Reckon there is *somethin' unnatural going on here.*

Chapter Ten
One Down, One to Go

Harlon's Pass didn't have a saloon nor a hotel as much as it had Hattie Cartwright.

The late-thirties widow experienced a set of particular circumstances resulting in her home serving as the town's only attempt at either. Considering a funeral went on, Zeb decided out of respect to give the people a little time before bothering them with a wanted notice. In a town as small as this one, it took merely walking in a straight line for less than a minute to see all of it.

Hattie's place sat at the approximate center of what passed for downtown. Hers was the largest house, the only one with three stories. The former parlor had been converted into a space similar to a saloon except for the lack of a bar, bartender, and obvious booze. A small sign advertising food and lodging convinced him to go inside and inquire.

After a brief introduction, Zeb took a seat at one of the half dozen tables, all covered in fine lavender fabric with fancy place settings. While not as lavish as the

Grand Mesa, it appeared the Widow Cartwright decided to use the family's 'fine China' on a daily basis rather than for special occasions. A pair of small, identical twin girls in white dresses sat together on the floor near the back of the room, happily playing with dolls. Both children stared at him when he walked in, took mere seconds to consider his presence, then smiled and waved before resuming their play as if he didn't exist.

He requested a meal and a room for the night, as well as inquired about lodging for Jasper. Upon learning the widow herself would tend to the horse, he insisted on doing it if she pointed him to the stable area. By the time he returned from situating the horse in the tiny two-stall stable behind the house, Hattie had set a plate of steak and potatoes on his table.

Much to Zeb's surprise, she asked to join him. Sensing her intent came from curiosity and a desire for conversation, he obliged. The woman possessed a distinct lack of shyness and, over the course of his meal, made lively conversation. By the time he'd finished eating, he'd learned Mr. Cartwright died three years ago to a fever-like illness when their daughters Flora and Fiona had been a mere one year old. Mr. Cartwright had also gone west with ideas of establishing a ranch, though unlike Zeb, he already had a wife and children. Also unlike Zeb, he possessed significant financial resources that allowed for him to start off building a giant house... *this* giant house.

Later, the Cartwrights disagreed on living arrangements—he preferred to be close to the ranch while she much favored the social connections of staying downtown. Their disagreement—and his decision to spend most of his time at the far-off ranch house—appeared to have spared her and the girls whatever sickness took him.

Having no interest in ranching, she sold the land and ranch house, which sat a few miles west of downtown. Having nowhere else to go, she remained here and essentially ran a hotel out of her home. She had the good fortune of being an adept cook, which resulted in a fairly regular business feeding those who worked too hard and long to make time to prepare food.

Being in a conversation with a woman who appeared to thrive on meeting people she'd never seen before made it impossible to resist asking about Arnold Parrish. Zeb took the wanted notice from his pocket and showed it to her.

"Have you seen this man around here?"

Hattie studied the blurry photographic print with the scrutiny of a Pinkerton detective. "I did not speak to him, but I do believe he was at Branch's yesterday."

"The dry goods store."

"Yes." Hattie handed him back the paper. "Two doors from my house to the right. Eugene Branch runs our general store."

Zeb re-folded the paper. "Yesterday. But not since?"

"No." She tugged at the thick lavender tablecloth to smooth a wrinkle. "I found it unusual a newcomer did not stop in here for something to eat. Most do. Hmm. Seems I was correct to assume he had something to hide."

"Indeed." Zeb regarded this almost-forty woman who both looked and acted younger than her age. The way she sat there staring at him like an eager child hearing stories reminded him of Heath. As such, she seemed quite likely to be well versed in the goings on around here. "What's your opinion the… unusual stories?"

Hattie leaned back, raising an eyebrow. "You're talking about what that little girl claims to have seen?"

Zeb rested his fork on the empty plate. "I'm of a mind to think the 'monster' this kid saw just might be the fella I'm looking for."

"Might be at that." Hattie nodded once. "All the strange stories are tied one way or another to the Lamb Ranch."

Zeb chuckled. "Someone out here raisin' sheep?"

"No, Mr. Clemens." Hattie suppressed a laugh. "The family's name is Lamb. You were having a conversation with the eldest son not long ago, Everett."

He couldn't recall seeing her earlier, neither in the funeral procession nor standing outside. Considering most of the town attended the funeral for Ollie, it stood out as somewhat strange she didn't go. Perhaps she'd been observing the event from her window and spotted a newcomer talking to the boy.

"Didn't notice you in the funeral group."

"Because I wasn't." Hattie fanned herself with a napkin. "Call it an odd superstition, but I prefer to distance myself from matters of death. Do you believe there is something after this world, Mr. Clemens?"

He cracked a half smile. "I've come to suspect such."

She relaxed, smiling. "Then you will perhaps not think me mad. I believe there is a veil of sorts that hangs between the living and the dead. The closer one gets to death, such as being near a body or a graveyard, or even a funeral, the thinner the veil."

Not having much opinion one way or the other thus far, Zeb merely nodded in acknowledgment.

"I had a dream soon after my husband Edmund's death that I am not entirely sure was a dream." Hattie glanced off to the side… for the first time since he'd met her appearing cautious or worried. "He stood at the foot of my bed, seeming angry… and I could somewhat see the wall right through his chest."

"What did he have to be angry with you about?" asked Zeb.

"Leaving him to die alone, I suspect." Hattie shifted her gaze back to him, making eye contact. "I refused to stay at the ranch house and kept our girls with me here. As I told you already, because of that, I am convinced we were spared whatever sickness took him. Edmund, or at least his spirit, seemed to feel we should have all been together to the very end."

"You mean die together?"

"Maybe. Anyway, these stories from the Lamb girl have me on edge, if I can be frank with you."

Zeb mulled this over. His experience with 'the angry dead' consisted entirely of fanciful things he'd read as a much younger man back East, all fictional stories intended to scare the reader. He'd regarded them as little more than someone taking the sorts of tales children told around a campfire and printing them. The notion a man could die to a sickness and become filled with anger over his fate didn't seem entirely without merit. After all, if a fiend like the one he encountered in Devil's Creek could be real, it opened the possibility that many more things people regarded as folklore might be as well.

From personal experience, Zeb didn't think death could change a man so much, but had to remember he hadn't truly died. Like a too-small fish, The Lady caught him and threw him back into the pond. Might it be possible the entity that little Ada Lamb claimed to have seen was the spirit of Hattie's deceased husband, Edmund Cartwright.

"Do you think this man you're after is still here?" asked Hattie.

"I'm inclined to, yes." Zeb eyed the afternoon light in the front windows, figuring he could get in a good few hours of searching before sunset. "Downtown's too small for him. He's not going to want to be anywhere a marshal or any lawman would find him right away. Best I reckon, he's either holed up on one of the ranches nearby or maybe even pitched a tent out in the sticks."

"There are a few places he might have made a camp," said Hattie. "Between town and my husband's former ranch property, there's a swath of junipers and firs. The trees cover a fair bit of land too rough for ranching or farming, but they're the only thing around here not wide open. If he's of a mind to stay hidden, he'd be there. Probably by one of the creeks."

"His associate said Arnold claimed to know someone around here."

"I find that unlikely." Hattie swiped a strand of dark hair off her face. "If anyone here had a son or brother given to robbing banks, we'd all know of it."

He shifted his jaw side to side. No reason to think Arnold wouldn't have lied about knowing someone here. Thieves didn't have to be honest with each other. "Maybe someone who hasn't been around here all that long? What sort of person bought your former husband's ranch?"

Hattie smoothed the tablecloth again. "Calvin Lamb."

Chapter Eleven
The Usual First Steps

Coincidences piling up often meant something.

Zeb stood outside Hattie's inn, surveying the town of Harlon's Pass while trying to make sense of things. A woman who seemingly lucked her way out of death by her refusal to live away from downtown lost her husband to an unexplained illness on the same property where a ranch hand was found dead with a caved-in head. The same ranch happened to be relatively close to the canyon where people found a Native American site so spooky it made the pastor relocate an entire graveyard. Taking a turn toward the strange, a young girl living there claimed to have seen a 'monster.'

He wondered if external powers guided him to Hattie to hear her story, but dismissed the notion. The tiny downtown had only one possible place for a traveler to go seeking food and/or a room. That he'd ended up talking to her had roughly the same odds of rain striking the ground after falling from a cloud. Arnold Parrish having an abrupt notion to come to this particular town remained strange enough to be questionable. Obviously, the man didn't have a normal sort of thinking process, otherwise he'd not be in the habit of robbing banks and shooting innocent people.

Up until he'd watched Arnold whack Rowena across the face, Zeb hadn't been a particularly strong adherent of the 'eye for an eye' mentality. However, he intended to give him at least one good knuckle sandwich for hitting the girl.

Harlon's Pass presented a problem disguised as a benefit. Being so dang small, it wouldn't take him long to check every building in the downtown. Alas, the same smallness all but guaranteed Arnold would not be anywhere nearby. Hattie didn't serve alcohol and the town lacked a proper saloon. With nowhere to drink or gamble, a man like Arnold had no reason to be among people who might see his face on a wanted notice.

He suspected the widow to be correct in her guess the bank robber would be camping out somewhere in the juniper forest to the west. She knew of no other people living here with the name Parrish. From where he stood, the distant woods looked fairly large. It would probably take him two or three days to search most of it.

In the interest of being proper and thorough, Zeb made his way around town showing Arnold's picture and asking everyone he met if they'd seen him. A few locals admitted to seeing him 'the other day' but only briefly. Not one person claimed to have ever seen him before or heard rumors about one of the outlying ranchers having a ne'er-do-well relative.

Eugene Branch, proprietor of the town's only general store, remembered him. He told Zeb that Arnold purchased a significant amount of canned goods and provisions, suggesting he planned to live rough for a while. Zeb didn't have a vast amount of experience chasing bank robbers, but the one's he'd heard of usually went straight to the nearest big town and lived large until the money ran out. Tracking down a bank robber who tried his best to disappear was a new beast he'd not yet encountered.

An outlaw who'd steal the kind of money Arnold got away with only to go crawl into a remote patch of woodlands and lay low seemed as strange as it did wise. Why steal all that money if he wouldn't use it for anything? On the other hand, spending it would increase the chances of being caught.

Seems I underestimated his smarts. Could be he's waitin' to get older so no one recognizes him. Zeb sighed. *Or something else pulled him out here.*

What small talk he'd made with people in the course of asking if anyone had seen Arnold often strayed into the stories coming from the Lamb Ranch. Those among the locals who didn't dismiss things of that nature attributed all the problems to whatever Native Americans had been in the area prior to the town being established. Every person who commented on it also mentioned the Lamb property was fairly close to the canyon where the Native artifacts had been discovered. A few even suggested a connection between them and Edmund Cartwright's mysterious death, blaming a 'curse.'

One rather agitated man by the name of Curtis Small believed the 'monster' the Lamb girl spotted was only 'one of them savages' dressed up. He also believed Ollie to have been murdered by a small group of Indians using stone-headed clubs, and wanted to gather up a bunch of men and 'go hunting.'

Zeb managed to calm the man down and send him

on his way after assuring him he would 'do whatever was necessary' to protect the townspeople. Of course, he had no intention to randomly shoot Natives. If, in fact, Ollie had been killed by one, it didn't feel like a sign of an impending invasion. Perhaps a Native or two snuck into town to steal things and got caught, then in a panic, killed the man who spotted them. If the Natives wanted to make war on Harlon's Pass, it would not have been one man killed in the middle of the night—and it also likely would have occurred years ago.

Too many possible explanations existed for him to attempt trying to understand it merely from standing there thinking. He had maybe six hours of daylight left, not enough to search all of the woods unless he planned on sleeping out there, which would be foolish. Even if no 'monster' or murderous Natives prowled the area, the woods still contained a bank robber who had no problem killing to avoid capture.

While death may have been a minor inconvenience for him, Zeb didn't feel like being robbed or shot.

Suppose I shall chase Arnold 'Coyote' Parrish in the morning.

At the sudden wonder if there might be a connection between Native American folklore and the man he chased, he frowned. What were the odds Arnold Parrish might not be a man at all but a manifestation of some trickster spirit the Natives believed in? What little he'd heard of it described a mischievous or evil entity the tribes knew as 'Coyote.' Depending on who told the story, it varied from a dark, malevolent entity to a wicked prankster. It had to be far more likely people gave Arnold the nickname 'Coyote' for being slippery and wily. The man didn't look as if he had the slightest trace of Native blood in him, so it made no sense for there to be a connection.

This, of course, didn't explain why Zeb had been seeing shaman spirits.

Grumbling to himself, he headed around back behind Hattie's to ready his horse.

Chapter Twelve
Chasing the Coyote

As much as Zeb tried not to dread possibly hunting 'the coyote spirit' rather than a man, he couldn't help but dwell on the idea.

Rumors of unexplained events were hardly uncommon out here. People had been subjected to years of brutal civil war as well as the economic hardship of losing everything. Many who migrated into the New Mexico territory had lost homes, land, and family to the battles. With all the memory of death and destruction fresh, no wonder a little girl's claim of seeing a monster managed to take hold in the minds of adults.

What is it about men that causes us to imagine the strangest explanation for somethin' we don't right away know about?

He chuckled to himself at the panic briefly set off back in Silver Mesa five months ago when someone discovered disturbed earth at the graveyard. What had likely been the work of grave robbers in the middle of the night got blamed on demons or possibly witches raising the dead. In hindsight, he found it particularly amusing since his new home town *did* in fact have a man who'd returned from the dead. He had not, however, needed to dig himself out of a coffin.

The thought made him cringe. He'd prefer permanent death to being trapped in a box underground. What would happen to him in that case? Would he continually suffocate only to wake up and suffocate again? Might The Lady somehow intercede to help him escape? What if she lacked the power to do so? Did he possess the strength to break out of a buried coffin? It seemed impossible.

More motivation not to get dead again.

Zeb rode west out from downtown Harlon's Pass, following a scrap of dirt road for about a quarter mile until it faded away. Not enough people made a regular habit of riding anywhere around here to imprint a permanent road on the land. Distant ranches to the left and right of the woods would likely need to be checked, eventually. However, based on their direction from town, he surmised them not to be the Lamb Ranch.

Again, he chuckled at the idea of someone raising baby sheep.

Unfortunate name for a rancher, that.

The inexplicable sense a connection existed between Arnold Parrish, the Native American spirits, and the strange goings on in town convinced him to start his search at the place where Hattie's husband died. Local resident, Curtis Small, believed wholly—and without any evidence whatsoever—an Indian killed Ollie. While Zeb brushed that aside as a product of prejudice, he considered the man might be correct in one regard: Ollie could very well have been killed by a man.

A very *normal* man by the name of Arnold Parrish.

WANTED: UNDEAD OR ALIVE

Zeb considered several possibilities. Arnold may have tried to break into the house to steal food or search for valuables. He might have been on the property to steal a horse if he'd run the one he had to death. Prior to the other day, Parrish hadn't been known as a threat to women or children. His grabbing Rowena seemed like a desperate act of convenience rather than a purposeful abduction of a young lady.

While he didn't believe Arnold to be the sort of crazed individual who'd kill a rancher and his family for amusement, Zeb certainly believed the man would kill anyone who got in his way. This notion urged the lawman to move faster, taking a relatively straight path through the juniper forest, not swerving around to search for a campsite.

He had to make sure the man he hunted didn't sow chaos upon an innocent family first.

The twisted juniper trees grew far enough apart from each other to afford him a reasonable ability to see around him. Without a culvert to hunker down in, a man would have to be sixty yards or so away in order to effectively hide. Despite his grim mission, the woods gave off a sense of serenity. A man capable of living without the vices of gambling, liquor, and prostitutes might be content to spend months or years here, hunting and fishing for food.

Nah. If he had a mind to live off the land, he'd not be robbin' banks.

No sign of a one-man campsite stood out from the woods within view of the path Zeb took. He and Jasper emerged again on open land some miles from the first trees. If anything, the trip truly illustrated the size of the forest he had to search. If Arnold became aware of his presence, the two might circle each other for weeks amid the junipers—assuming the thief didn't slip away and leave Zeb searching empty woods.

As soon as he emerged from the forest, Zeb breathed a sigh of relief. The property he assumed to be the Lamb Ranch—directly in front of him about another half mile —appeared active. Men, cows, and a few horses moved about the land. A nice, though smaller and more plain house than the one Hattie lived in, sat at the approximate center of the property, near a creek that fed into the woods from the rocky hills further west. A second, smaller house stood about a hundred feet away from the main structure.

The canyon the townspeople so feared lurked in the distance well past the ranch, hazed by low hanging clouds. If he kept on riding without stopping at the house, it would be dark before he made it there. Of course, he had better things to do than chase curiosity over what manner of Native artifacts could so frighten townspeople they'd relocate an entire graveyard.

Nothing about this place makes a lick of sense. He shook his head. *Who digs up three dozen graves because someone found some cave paintings?*

"This guy better damn sure be a normal man. I ain't about to chase no Coyote Spirit across the West."

Zeb grumbled at the thought. He needed to stop letting his strange experiences make him assume *every-9thing* had a connection to the unknown. Here, he simply had an ordinary bank robber hiding from a not-so-ordinary marshal.

Focusing his thoughts entirely on the mundanity of a lawman tracking a robber, he rode across the field to the ranch house. A skinny little blonde girl of around eight sat in the shade of the porch having a tea party with three rag dolls, a ceramic owl, and a wooden duck. The dirt-covered, barefoot little girl in a dingy hand-me-down of a dress, looked like a street urchin but spoke to the toys in the manner of an aristocrat.

When Zeb approached the house, she paused in addressing Count Owl to look at him, instantly dropping the fake high-society affect to giggle and wave.

"Hi!" chirped the girl. "I'm Ada. Who are you?"

Zeb tipped his hat to her, dismounted his horse and walked up to the stairs, where he took a knee closer to her eye level. "Name's Zebadiah."

"Hello, Mr. Zebadiah." Ada pointed at his badge. "Are you a sheriff?"

"I'm a marshal." He winked. "It's like a sheriff, 'cept I don't have ta stay in only one town."

"Are you here to take the monster to jail?" Ada blinked, then scrunched up her nose in confusion. "Wait. Do monsters go to people jail, or do you have monster jail?"

Zeb grinned. "Oh, there's a special monster jail. Can't put them in people jails. They don't get along well with the other bad guys."

Ada giggled again.

"I hear you've seen this monster."

The girl nodded eagerly, making her hair flop all over the place. "Yes."

"When did you see it?"

She fidgeted, tapping her big toes together. "A few nights ago."

"Shouldn't a little girl like you be asleep at night?"

"I wake up a lot at night 'cause I hear stuff." Ada grinned. "My brothers, Ev and Grover, don' like wakin' up. Pa has ta drag 'em outta bed in the morning mos' times."

Zeb nodded. "You heard something at night and

woke up?"

"Yes." The child's grin faded to a serious expression. She lowered her voice almost to a whisper. "It was just outside. I peeked it from the window."

"Can you tell me what it looked like?"

She nodded. "Yes."

Zeb waited. The child said nothing.

"*Will* you tell me what it looked like?" asked Zeb.

"Okay." Ada covered her mouth to hold back another giggle. "The monster pretended to be a man, but it's not a man."

"Two legs, two arms, one head?"

Ada scrambled to her feet. "It walked like this." She hunched forward, head tilted to one side, arms somewhat raised. The child proceeded to shuffle across the porch as if her legs and arms had become stiff with rigor mortis. She moaned, made a pawing gesture at nothing, and then dropped the act, standing up straight. "Like that."

"Could it have been a man pretending to be a monster?" asked Zeb.

"I don't think so." Ada dropped to sit on the top porch step. "People aren't s'posed ta be that color. White like mama's curtains. He looked like a dead person what's been in a field for a couple a' days. An' the monster had candles for eyes."

Zeb regarded this tiny sprite of a girl who claimed to have seen a walking dead man with glowing eyes and… yet didn't seem the least bit afraid of him. To make matters worse, she apparently knew what a corpse left in a field looked like. Women and children ought to be spared such sights as far as he was concerned.

The door behind the girl opened, revealing a strawberry blonde woman in her early thirties who so closely resembled Ada they had to be mother and daughter. Mrs. Lamb also wore a dress, one in a much better state of repair than the child's. Her shoes looked well-worn but hardly pauperish. Mrs. Lamb stared at Zeb with an expression of guarded hesitation.

Ada turned to look behind her. "Mama, Mr. Zebadiah's here to arrest the monster. He's like a sheriff but for everywhere."

The woman's defensiveness faded to confusion. She appeared to notice the badge on his vest, then relaxed before sighing. "I'm sorry my daughter's wild stories caused a stir bad enough the marshals sent someone out this way."

Zeb stood, dusted off his knee, then tipped his hat to her. "Deputy U.S. Marshal Zebadiah Clemens." He offered a hand. "I'm not here to arrest any monsters, but if I happen to come across one, I'll certainly do what I can."

The woman descended the porch steps to stand on the dirt before shaking his hand. "Isabelle Lamb."

"Pleasure to make your acquaintance," said Zeb.

Mrs. Lamb looked him up and down. "If you aren't here because of Ada's imagination, what brings a marshal all the way out here?"

Ada rolled her eyes and mouthed, "Is not imagination."

Another girl, roughly the same age as Rowena, walked into view inside the house, carrying a basket full of wet clothing. She stared across the parlor and out the open front door at Zeb for a moment with a 'who's that?' expression before shrugging and walking away deeper into the home.

"Nothin' so fancy as monsters. I'm looking for a man who robbed a bank." Zeb pulled the wanted notice out and held it up. "Have either of you seen this man?"

Mrs. Lamb shook her head. "Can't say I have."

"No," said Ada.

The child's complete lack of reaction to the picture should have made Zeb feel relief. It had the opposite effect. Sure, he considered it good that a dangerous bank robber hadn't been anywhere near her. However, it also meant whatever 'monster' she saw had not been Arnold Parrish lurking around. How much of her description came from reality and how much came from a child's imagination, he had no way to tell. If moonlight caught someone's eyes at the right angle, they could seem to glow. A freak reflection wouldn't explain why a person shambled about like a living corpse nor *looked* like a body left outside for a few days.

Maybe her monster was simply a nightmare?

"You shouldn't bother the marshal with talk of monsters," said Mrs. Lamb in a scolding tone.

Ada held her arms out to either side. "But someone's gotta stop the monsters from doing bad things."

Mrs. Lamb sighed, staring apologetically at him.

"It's all right." Zeb waved dismissively. "Ada's not causing any trouble. Didn't hear word of anything strange until I arrived in town. It's possible the 'haunting' your daughter observed is the bank robber I'm looking for skulking about after dark. Has anything else odd happened around here?"

Little Ada stared up at him, her serious expression almost comical on someone so small. "I didn't see no bank robber. I saw a monster. Plain and simple!"

Mrs. Lamb patted the girl on the head. "Go play, sweetie."

Zeb smiled at her. "I'm inclined to believe you."

Grinning, Ada scrambled off the porch and ran off

into the field. She made it only about twenty paces before tripping and sliding on her chest, getting a face full of dirt and likely adding another small rip or two to her dress. Without any hesitation or tears, the girl bounced back up and kept running like nothing happened.

Zeb chuckled, watching her race off. "Lot of energy in that one."

"Too much." Mrs. Lamb sighed. "She's a handful. All the rambunctiousness my boys should have had, she got. Times, I wish she'd be more like her older sister Mae. I saw your look, Deputy Clemens. Before you judge us too harshly, the dress she's wearing was good as new last month. She's rough on everything except her dolls. Wants to learn how to shoot now. God help us."

He whistled.

"Well…" Mrs. Lamb smoothed her hands down the front of her own dress. "Aside from a child's flights of fancy, there have admittedly been some strange things going on lately."

"Strange how?"

The woman leaned against the column holding up the roof spur over the porch steps. "Vandalism mostly. Busted doors. Broken window. A fence smashed. My husband, Calvin, thinks it's the work of cougars or bears or something. Norman and Jesse say they heard someone walking around outside the house after dark. They got wind of Ada's wild stories, though you'd think grown men would have the sense not to listen to a nine-year-old's opinion on monsters."

"I see."

Mrs. Lamb pointed at another house some hundred yards away. "The men who work for us sleep there. Can't say anything's come around the family house except for whatever Ada thinks she saw at night." The woman paused, seeming worried.

"Something else?" Zeb raised an eyebrow.

"Well, there's the unfortunate death of our ranch hand, which I'm sure you've heard about by now."

Zeb nodded.

"And last month, one of our hired men went missing. He's young enough to maybe be surprised at how much work the job involved. It's possible he simply quit and left without saying anything… except for…"

"For what?"

"I don't want to make Ada's imaginative stories seem any more real, but…" Mrs. Lamb folded her arms. "You'd think if a man was going to quit and run off, he'd not leave all his things in his room, right? No one saw him leave, and he left with only the clothes on his back. Calvin thinks he maybe went off to try fishin' in the creek or some such thing and something happened to him. Do you think he ran into your bank robber?"

"How long has he been missing?"

"Three weeks?" Mrs. Lamb squinted at the sky. "Maybe four. I can barely even remember the poor boy's name."

Zeb shook his head. "The man I'm after wouldn't have been around these parts that long ago. What's he look like?"

"He's gotta be around twenty-two, but has a baby face." She gestured at the house used by the ranch hands. "Jesse's our foreman. He'd know the young man's name. My sons likely would, too. They spend most of their time here, helping out and working."

"All right. I'll try not to make a nuisance of myself then. Pleasure speaking with you. If you do see the man on the notice or anything else you think I might need to look into, I'll be staying at Hattie's for the next couple o' days."

"All right. Thank you, marshal."

Zeb again tipped his hat. The woman walked into the house, leaving the front door open. He stepped away from the porch, glancing back and forth between the ranch hands' house and the distant juniper forest. Random acts of vandalism did sound plausible as the work of a large wild animal—or a disoriented, confused, or enraged monster.

Regardless of all the things he didn't know, he had several facts front and center. First, *something* lurked in the area of the Lamb Ranch. And second, that said something probably killed Ollie. Third, it stood to reason to credit the random destruction of various structures and items on the property to the same entity.

Sheesh. How much calamity could befall one place? The simplest explanation would be a single cause. Mrs. Lamb made a good point. A man intending to quit a job much more demanding than expected wouldn't walk away and leave the bulk of his worldly possessions behind.

I don't believe Ollie was the first man to die here.

Well, whatever oddity plagued the ranch, he could always come back to deal with later.

For now, he had a bank robber to catch.

Chapter Thirteen
A Strange Demise

Zeb rode into the forest, having made two decisions.

His first decision was to pursue Arnold before worrying about any supernatural problems in Harlon's Pass. The Lady had not appeared to him nor given him any strong sense of urgency. Of course, she also hadn't explicitly told him to go to Devil's Creek until after he'd largely ignored several hints of increasingly less subtlety.

If she wants me to do things, why she's gotta be obtuse about it?

Grumbling, Zeb scanned the woods. He didn't know if Arnold had become aware of his presence or if he expected anyone to track him here. In an ideal world, the man would be complacent and believe he'd gotten away without a trace. After all, he likely earned his nickname of Coyote for being sneaky—or lucky. Often times, an outlaw's ability to evade the authorities came down to dumb luck more than skill or ability.

The second decision he made was to throw caution

to the wind and sleep in the forest if his search continued into the dark. Which seemed likely, since he did not expect to be so lucky as to find Arnold before the sun went down.

Roughly two hours into his meandering back-and-forth walk, he caught a whiff of the unmistakable stink of dead body. He turned toward the source of the odor and soon happened upon a shallow creek that appeared to be the same waterway passing through the middle of the Lamb Ranch. Not far from the water, tucked inside a cluster of three closely spaced trees, lay a set of human remains decayed to little more than exposed bones partially trapped in a miasma of liquefied flesh.

The area had no evidence of a fire pit nor tent nor bedroll, so whoever the dead man was, he couldn't have been camping here. The corpse also appeared too far gone to possibly be Arnold Parrish, who would only have arrived in this area a day or two ago at most.

Zeb dismounted and walked over to the remains, as close as his stomach could tolerate the odor. Flies swarmed the corpse, dashing off and landing on the fleshy parts in an endless cycle. The skull resembled a clay pot someone smashed with a rock. The left wall of the skull appeared the most intact, while the rest of it had broken apart into fragments. No sign of the jaw lay anywhere in sight.

Zeb pictured a man sleeping on the ground while another man smashed a small boulder down upon his head. Such a cowardly attack could cause damage like what he observed here. Though, it wouldn't explain why the jaw disappeared. Dark splatter on one of the trees resembled dried blood—and quite a lot of it. He rose to stand, eyeing the splatter. As much as he hated the implication of what his eyes told him, he suspected this man died while upright rather than being ambushed in his sleep.

Something had hit him so hard his skull burst open. The jaw likely went flying from the force of the strike. Following a hunch, Zeb walked past the bloodstained tree, searching for the missing jawbone he suspected would be on the ground a distance away from the rest of the remains. Alas, he didn't find it, though considered it possible some manner of wildlife scavenger picked it up and ran off.

"Gonna guess you're that missing ranch hand…" Zeb turned in place, looking around. "Don't suppose your spirit's still around and wants to tell me what the Sam Hill happened."

Except for the sickly-sweet stench of a rotten body, the woods still gave off an air of placidity, but no ghostly voices.

"Seems not. Rest in peace, whoever you were." He walked back over and crouched beside the bones. "Forgive me for not seeing to a more proper rest for you right this moment. Got a bad man to find first. Wait here. I'll be back."

Zeb returned to his horse and climbed up onto the saddle, shaking his head. *Going to be smelling this poor bastard for weeks. Damn sure hope Ada didn't see this guy.*

After a brief look around to get his bearings, he headed southeast, hoping to find some sign of his quarry...

Chapter Fourteen
Too Damn Dark

Even before his life took a turn for the strange, Zeb occasionally experienced eerie feelings of not being alone, as though a threatening presence lurked somewhere nearby.

He suspected such moments to be a normal part of life, though had no understanding nor explanation for what caused them. More than likely, he reckoned humans possessed a much weaker ability to sense danger than animals and too much 'smarts' to listen to it. The same way deer picked up on subtle noises or smells betraying the approach of a predator, people likely did too. Animals, lacking the human need to convince themselves they'd only imagined things, ran like hell the instant something spooked them.

Episodes of unexplained fear hadn't been terribly common for him since childhood.

He couldn't point to any specific moments that stood out in his mind, merely the vague recollection of being alone in the dark and getting the distinct notion something else had been there, something he ought not to trust. More than likely it had been nothing more than the imagination of a boy playing with the common insecurities of a child who knew little of how the world worked. Becoming randomly frightened for no apparent reason in dark rooms or while alone in the woods was something he assumed happened to most children. He couldn't by rights claim to have had a similar experience after becoming an adult.

Until now.

Zeb stopped riding among the junipers so as to avoid making any noise. Jasper seemed nervous as well. The forest, which had been entirely peaceful up until sunset, changed once darkness fell. Though he knew beyond a doubt he remained awake, the shift in mood came as rapidly as a dream turning to a nightmare without warning.

It ain't Arnold puttin' me on edge. That's for damn sure.

He shook his head, dismissing his nervousness as a folly. Spending a while talking to a child who claimed to have seen a dead man wandering around got his mind wrapped around such ideas. Surely, the little one had to be imagining things. No girl her age could've seen such a thing and spoken of it so calmly—or so he thought. As rambunctious as the girl might be according to her mother, he had to think the sight of a fiend outside the natural order of life and death would have frightened her. For a moment, he felt foolish at being more on edge than a nine-year-old.

Fine line between careful and a'feared.

He looked around at the darkness, seeing only scattered traces of forest where scraps of moonlight pierced the leaves to shine on tree trunks. The sense of a presence in the woods nearby came most strongly from behind.

After a minute or so of sitting completely still and hearing nothing, Zeb urged Jasper to walk. As if he also sensed something wrong, the horse crept forward trying to stay quiet. Mere seconds later, a rustle came from the weeds an instant before a soft *thump*.

Zeb figured someone followed about fifty feet behind him, slightly to the left. He assumed the thump came from an inopportune root or rock nearly tripping the man and making him take a hard, unexpected step. A noise like that might make an ambusher realize they've blown their cover and charge. With that in mind, Zeb kept walking the horse forward, not reacting to the sound other than to rest a hand on his gun.

The man stalking him stepped heavily a second time.

Arnold is either the clumsiest sumbitch in the West or he's drunk.

Zeb continued moving while listening to the obvious sounds of a man staggering among the trees. Branches cracked, detritus on the ground crunched underfoot, and the occasional heavy stomp kept pace with him. Each minute that passed convinced him more and more his imagination got the better of him earlier. It was nothing more worrisome than an inebriated bank robber shadowing him. He peered back at a forest saturated in blackness. At present, even the scraps of moonlight had vanished.

At the thought of how odd it would be for a drunk man to be able to follow him in such darkness, Zeb steered to his right. Unable to see much, he trusted Jasper to avoid walking into trees. Bafflingly, the unseen man altered course to follow, even though it should not have been possible for him to see.

All right, pal. Enough of this.

A tree materialized into view up ahead, barely visible thanks to a bit of moonlight finding a gap in the leaves. He hadn't noticed any trace of it until being close enough to spit on it. Zeb tugged Jasper to a stop and jumped down from the saddle. As he took cover behind the tree, his horse appeared to understand his plan and resumed walking. Perhaps the animal merely meandered off in search of something to munch on, but he sure seemed to be purposefully helping him set up an ambush.

Zeb lay in wait, gun poised, staring into the darkness in the direction of the stumbling stalker. Between the hairs on the back of his neck standing up, simmering anger over Arnold's mistreatment of Rowena, and the simple desire to get out of the forest to a comfortable bed, he was tempted to simply shoot Arnold as soon as the outlaw came into view.

The crunching of leaves drew his gaze to a particular spot in the dark.

Zeb aimed.

For a few seconds, he stared at the inky morass of night in his gunsights. Then something moved. Zeb focused on the spot and managed to make out the basic shape of a slightly hunched-over man in dark attire. Though he couldn't see any detail whatsoever, he somehow knew he did not gaze upon the man he hunted. This figure appeared taller and thicker than Arnold "Coyote" Parrish.

The unknown man lumbered off to the side rather than directly toward him.

Zeb watched the figure for the span of three breaths. Rather than stalking Zeb, the shadowy traveler appeared to be moving in a similar direction at a languid pace, as if he and the lawman were simply following a well-worn trail. Except no obvious trail ran through here. Also, this didn't explain why the man had stopped when Zeb stopped, or why the stranger seemed to turn to follow when Zeb changed course.

However, it didn't appear as if the man cared to have any direct business with him.

Zeb released the hammer on his Colt, easing it forward with a faint *click*. The tiny sound in the unnaturally still forest seemed as loud as a gunshot. The shambling silhouette abruptly looked toward him, revealing two bright orange spots alight with the intensity of candle flames.

Somehow, Zeb managed not to emit a noise of surprise.

The strange figure's eyes gave off enough light for the lawman to make out the corpse-white skin of a square-faced man with a short, black beard. After a momentary stare, the entity gave a distasteful grunt, as though regarding food he had no interest in touching and turned away.

Zeb swallowed. Yeah, the man looked dead as all get out.

The kid was right.

A normal human response to the sight of an animated corpse—running like hell—instinctively crossed Zeb's mind. However, he held still for a few seconds more, allowing his thoughts to catch up to the reality of his situation.

Guess The Lady did send me here after all. In her own roundabout way.

He gave a brief sigh, then hurried off in pursuit of the creature. It—or he—didn't appear interested in harming Zeb, but that didn't prove it wouldn't hurt anyone else. As of the moment, too many questions remained for him to be able to decide what to do beyond following it.

Zeb rushed through the forest, bumping into trees and branches in his haste to catch up to the mysterious creature. Fear gave way to the drive of a hunter stalking after a wounded deer. He abandoned caution or any attempt to be stealthy, both arms up to shield his face from trees appearing out of the blackness without warning while chasing the ever distant crunch of a stumbling monster.

Moments later, it occurred to him all noise had faded away but for what he made.

Zeb stopped and cocked an ear. Only the rush of his heavy breaths disturbed the otherwise perfect silence. The stumbling figure shouldn't have been able to outrun him, yet it had. He turned to look behind him at nothingness. Certainly, the entity could have simply stopped moving and ducked. If so, it would have been easy to miss in such murky darkness.

This ain't gonna end well. It's too damn dark. It's time not to be a fool.

"Jasp," said Zeb. "Where ya be?"

A nicker came from the distance on his right.

"Damn horse has more sense than I do."

Shaking his head, Zeb holstered his Colt and trudged toward the sounds of his steed, somewhere in the dark.

Chapter Fifteen
Bunch o' Nonsense

Best Zeb could figure, he made it back to Hattie's place around midnight.

A separate door on the back left side of the building led directly to a hallway containing the rooms she rented out in the manner of a hotel. He ignored it for the moment to get Jasper settled in the small stable. Once finished, Zeb headed inside. He made it within five steps of his room before another door at the far end of the corridor abruptly swung open. An impossibly tall, dark silhouette loomed in the doorway, surrounded by glowing light.

Zeb froze, staring. Though his heart may have stopped for a beat or two, his expression didn't show it. As the shadowy form moved closer it shrank. He soon realized lantern shadow made an ordinary woman seem seven feet tall in the dark.

Hattie Cartwright, dressed in a heavy cloak over what appeared to be her nightclothes, glided toward him as noiseless as a phantom, her expression confused. Like a mother catching their son sneaking in too late, she fixed him with an inquisitive stare as to what in tarnation he was doing out and about at such an hour. Most likely, the woman who lived in perpetual fear of her dead husband's ghost coming after her and her children did not sleep soundly.

"Pardon, ma'am," said Zeb a trace over a whisper. "Didn't mean to wake you."

"It's all right. I worried when you weren't inside after dark. Happy to see you're all right." She leaned back, smiling to herself. "Chasing monsters?"

"Chasin' a fugitive, mostly. Ordinary man, but I've heard some tales."

Hattie pursed her lips. "Yes, there are tales around these parts. People getting odd feelings. Other people saying they've seen things. Animals turning up dead. Things broken. Depending on who's telling the tale, it's everything from cougars to coyotes to one o' them skinwalkers the Natives speak of."

Zeb couldn't claim to know much at all about 'skinwalkers' other than the Natives regarded them with a great deal of fear and trepidation. Even speaking the word could frighten some of them into silence.

Zeb removed his hat. "I'm guessin' the truth is somewhere in the middle."

"You'd likely be right." Hattie smiled. "Most around here think that skinwalker stuff's a bunch o' nonsense, but I'm not so sure. What about you, marshal?"

He glanced down at his hat, debating the wisdom of sharing what he'd seen. The woman had plenty of ghost stories in her head and likely didn't need anything else to be frightened of. "Well, I don't want to say it's complete rubbish. A Native sees a steam train, they goin' ta think it's some manner of fire-breathing monster on account of not understandin' how machines work, right?"

"Aye, that's my thought. Might'a been something after all, but who can say?" Hattie fiddled at her lantern, making it a little brighter. "The unusual things going on here in town are probably the work of wild animals."

"Could be." Zeb grasped the doorknob to his room.

"What are you fixin' to do tomorrow?" asked Hattie while turning to walk off.

"Reckon I'll be hunting a Coyote." He nodded once to her.

"Wild animals?"

Zeb frowned at the way the miscreant treated Rowena as well as struck Janie Brennan. "More or less, yeah. Wild animal on two legs."

She gave a faint sigh. "You be careful out there. Too many have died around here already."

"I will. Good night, ma'am," said Zeb.

"Night, marshal."

He watched her drift off through the door at the far end of the hall, then close it. The soft click of a lock followed. It didn't feel like a statement of distrust toward him, considering she ran a hotel and the front door remained unlocked. After all, anyone from guest to vagrant to angry spirit might walk in at any time. Or even the walking dead.

With a sigh, he entered the bedroom... and locked the door behind him, too.

Chapter Sixteen
Gambling

Morning arrived with an unexpected benefit: invitation to breakfast.

Evidently, Hattie made a habit of providing meals with her rooms. Zeb got the sense she did the same for all guests and not out of some attempt to ingratiate herself to a prospective new husband. The woman appeared quite happy to be on her own and in no hurry to change her living arrangements. Perhaps she worried the theoretical angry ghost of her former husband would become enraged with jealousy?

Since he hadn't yet seen any sign of another adult in the place, he assumed she had done the cooking… unusual for a woman from the upper class. The meal was pleasant except for the oddity of the twin four-year-old daughters staring at him the whole time they ate. Cute as dolls, the girls reacted as if they'd never seen another human being before, observing him the way one might watch a strange bird.

Neither child spoke, nor did they appear fearful—

merely curious.

He had a brief conversation with Hattie, who sat and ate breakfast with him, in regard to his plans to spend the day hunting for Arnold. As Harlon's Pass lacked any sort of sheriff's office or jailhouse, he intended to begin the trip back to Silver Mesa right away if he managed to find the man. If not, he'd return to spend one more night here. After breakfast, she packed him something to eat for lunch, then bid him good luck and goodbye in case he did not return.

"What the heck did I see last night?" he asked no one in particular.

Out in the middle of the scrubland between downtown and the trees, he didn't expect an answer as much as hope The Lady might decide to send him a clue. He still hadn't seen anything to suggest she had sent him here deliberately to protect the locals from a supernatural fiend. However, seeing something almighty weird lurking in the woods where at least two men had been killed certainly implied he ought to act.

He stopped to eat a little past noon, sitting on a rock by a creek so shallow a three-year-old couldn't swim in it. It still offered water for him and Jasper to drink, and the shade of nearby junipers proved relaxing. It seemed scarcely possible he sat in the same forest he'd been in last night when the strange entity appeared to follow him. Nothing about the peaceful scenery gave away the slightest clue anything could be wrong here.

Distracted by thoughts of the unexplained shadowy figure, Zeb continued wandering the junipers. The forest couldn't have been more than four miles across east-to-west and maybe a mile or so thick north-to-south, yet it seemed endless to him.

As twilight approached, Zeb realized he ached

everywhere. It had been a while since he'd spent so many hours in a row atop a horse. Even at an unhurried walking pace, riding all day left the inside of his legs stiff and sore from being in the same position.

Gonna be dark soon. Zeb peered up through the leaves at the sky. There couldn't be that much more ground to search. That he hadn't found Arnold yet implied the man either left the area or hadn't been here to begin with. He assumed Arnold must have somehow noticed him and slipped away. *Maybe he* does *have kin here no one realized. Tomorrow, I'll check around the other ranches.*

Right about the moment he decided to call it quits and head back to Hattie's, a whiff of food came by on the breeze. Zeb stopped his horse and sniffed at the air.

Baked beans.

Careful to make as little sound as possible, he eased himself down from the saddle, then patted the horse on the neck.

"Wait here, boy," he whispered.

Zeb brushed at Jasper's mane, pulling his hand away with a few stray hairs dangling from his fingers. He held his arm out, observing the way the horsehairs fluttered to determine the direction from which the wind carried the aroma of roasting beans and wood smoke. Gun drawn, he advanced.

Soon, the soft crackle of a fire reached his ears. A few minutes of walking later, Zeb spotted a campsite where a small tent stood beside a fallen tree. One man sat on the tree, tending to a sad little cook fire heating a single tin can hung on a wire over the flames.

After sneaking up as close as he could without being seen, Zeb took cover behind a tree and peered around it. At this distance, even with the man's back turned, it couldn't have been more obvious he'd gotten lucky. Arnold Parrish still wore the same dingy off-red shirt and dark pants he'd had on the day of the robbery. Admittedly, it had only been a few days, so finding the man wearing the same garments didn't come as a major surprise.

The outlaw seemed relaxed as could be, unbothered by whatever strange entity lurked in these woods, as well as any worry about the law finding him. In fact, he appeared ever so slightly annoyed, as if he resented having a small fortune while being unable to use any of it out in the middle of nowhere.

Money's fickle like that. Some great joke men play on themselves, killin' each other for bits of paper that don' mean nothin' when you're out here in the boonies. Can't buy off a hungry cougar… or whatever that thing was I saw last night.

The terrified scream Rowena let out when she believed she'd been thrown to her death echoed in Zeb's memory. He raised his gun and drew a bead on the back of Arnold's head.

Damn tempting, but that ain't me. He'll hang soon enough.

"Arnold Parrish!" bellowed Zeb.

The man gave a startled squawk akin to the noise that might come out of a chicken punted by a horse. He leapt from the fallen tree to land sprawled on the ground beside the cook fire, facing away from Zeb.

"Jesus, Mary, and Joseph," rasped the outlaw. "Don't do that. You scared the life out of me."

"Well, if you wanna keep holdin' onto that life, I suggest you stand up real slow like." Zeb kept his aim on the man. "Bounty on you's good alive or dead. After what you did to that little girl, I'd just as soon have the easier time o' transportin' a body."

Arnold sighed at the sky, then peered back over his shoulder at Zeb. "Ah, come now. Her old man's gotta hit her worse n' 'at."

"Her *old man* don't make a habit of tossing her over cliffs." Zeb scowled. The idea of mild Hilmer Paine raising a hand to his daughter or his wife at all seemed ludicrous.

The outlaw pushed himself up from being prone to a kneeling position. "She bit me!"

Zeb damn near shot him in the leg for using the weak excuse he fully expected to hear, but didn't want to waste the bullet in case he needed it for something else. "Save it. Don't do nothin' stupid now."

"Well now, marshal." Arnold chuckled. "I'm a gambling sort of man."

"I ain't here to play cards."

"Oh, you misunderstand me," said Arnold. "Why would I take a sure loss when I have chance on my side?"

Before Zeb could reply, a gunshot went off. The bullet embedded in the tree he hid behind—a remarkably accurate shot for a man quick-drawing and firing from the hip. Flinching at the sudden attack cost Zeb a kill shot. His bullet hit dirt as Arnold scrambled to take cover on the ground behind the fallen tree he'd been sitting on. No part of him peeked out as a target. Of course, he had nowhere to go.

Zeb took the opportunity to dash to a different tree so he wouldn't be where Arnold last saw him. Sure enough, the man poked his hand over the tree and shot at the lawman's former location. Zeb returned fire, missing the hand but coming close enough to probably give him a splinter or four. Seconds later, Arnold peeked around the right end of the tree. Zeb fired hastily, trying to hit the man before he could duck back. Arnold appeared to have similar plans. Both men fired at the same instant. Both missed—and slipped out of sight.

"Why ya gotta be a damn fool?" called Zeb.

"Ain't foolish." Arnold's rapid breathing filled a few seconds of quiet. "If I surrender and go with you, I'm as good as dead. If I kill you, my problems go away."

"Don't count on that," said Zeb.

The lawman frowned. He couldn't argue the logic there. Widespread use of the death penalty didn't leave much reason for outlaws to give up. Any man smart enough to realize surrendering peacefully to the marshal wouldn't stop a judge from sentencing them to hang would do everything possible to avoid being taken into custody.

A shot rang out from Arnold's direction, striking the tree inches above Zed's face. The bullet careened off into the distance with a high-pitched squeal.

"Tarnation!" shouted Zeb, ducking the spray of wood fragments.

Arnold shot again, missing the tree entirely.

Zeb recovered and snapped off two shots before the man scooted back behind the log again.

"Damn," howled Arnold, laughing. "We're both shootin' like a pair of drunken idiots."

Gun smoke hung over the campsite, neither man moving, speaking, or shooting. Zeb kept his Colt trained on the fallen tree, ready to shoot the first hint of the man to present itself.

"The hell are you doin' out here anyway?" called Arnold. "Just a damn bank robbery. Ain't like it's your money. Ain't even all that much."

Zeb shifted his jaw side to side. "You really want to

know?"

"Seein' as how one of us ain't likely to be breathin' an hour from now, sure, lawdog. Enlighten me."

"The girl. If you boys had just skedaddled outta town without kidnapping a child, good chance I wouldn't have been motivated enough to follow you out this damn far. Minute you decided to throw her into the ravine, you guaranteed I'm gonna hunt you until one of us is dead."

"How noble of you, marshal." Arnold laughed. "I'll put that on your gravestone. Here lies a marshal. Dead because he's noble."

"Poetic plan, but you're gonna be disappointed," muttered Zeb.

Arnold reached his gun hand up over the top of the log. Zeb dashed to his left, ducking low. At the rapid thumping of Zeb's footfalls, the outlaw decided to pop up for a look. When he did, Zeb pivoted and fired on the run, gouging the wood a few inches shy of Arnold's chin.

The man ducked. Zeb crashed into a tree, flattening himself against it for cover.

"Hah!" called Arnold. "You missed again. By my count, you got one bullet left."

Zeb thumbed his second Colt on his left hip, still full. "So what if I do?"

A crunch in the woods drew his attention. Zeb peered around his tree toward Arnold's position. The forest had become abruptly dark, much more so than it had been mere seconds earlier. In the shadowy haze behind the bank robber's campsite stood a silhouetted figure, almost entirely black save for two small points of bright orange light where its eyes should be.

Ah, hell.

He didn't know one way or the other if being killed by such a creature changed what happened to a man's soul in whatever afterlife awaited them. Could be it made no difference if Arnold died to a hangman's noose, Zeb's bullet, or that creature… but he didn't like taking the chance. Bad enough the man would be sentenced to die for killing several people, mostly bystanders at banks he'd robbed and lawmen. He didn't deserve to have his soul consumed—or whatever this thing intended to do.

"Behind you," called Zeb.

Arnold laughed. "How dumb do you think I am?"

"Dumb enough to rob banks and shoot people, but that ain't got nothin' to do with it." Zeb pointed. "I ain't trying to trick you. There's a whole lot o' badness comin' up on ya."

Something in his tone of voice must have been convincing. Arnold risked peeking up over the tree at him, then twisted to look behind him. The instant he spotted the creature, it charged at him. Arnold let out a scream of dread, scrambling crab-like to climb over the fallen tree, no longer the least bit concerned it left him wide open to being shot.

The entity caught him by his ankles, dragging him backward. Arnold lost his grip on his weapon in his frantic—and futile—attempt to claw at the dirt to stop himself from being hauled into the creature's grip. The figure pulled him upright, holding him by the throat with a single pale hand. Arnold emitted the squeak of a man trying to scream with no air in his lungs.

Zeb stepped out of cover, drawing his second gun—and emptied all six shots into the glowing-eyed man.

As if he'd shot an incorporeal ghost, the entity showed no reaction whatsoever to the bullets. It did, however, seem to forget about Arnold and turned to stare at Zeb.

Zeb glanced down at his guns. They'd worked on the beast in Devil's Creek.

Well… suppose it'd be too much to ask for bullets to work on all *this nonsense, wouldn't it?*

Out of spite, he fired the last bullet from his right-hand gun into the creature's forehead. It left a small, black hole that disappeared in only a few seconds.

"You're gonna be a chore, aren't ya?" muttered Zeb.

The pale-faced man tossed Arnold aside like a forgotten toy, faced Zeb, and began walking toward him.

Ah, hell.

Zeb raised both guns, briefly forgetting neither one had any bullets left. He sighted over them at a cluster of holes in the man's dark shirt; proof his bullets *did* hit something solid, but had little effect. The entity closed in, drawing back an arm to wallop Zeb. This close, he ceased appearing to be a creature made mostly of shadows, seeming quite solid—and dead. Orange light shone from within glassy eyeballs, as if a lantern wick burned inside them. A few signs of decay ringed the eyes, nostrils, and mouth… but for the most part, the body looked like one laid out on an undertaker's slab: freshly dead.

Backpedaling, Zeb ducked the man's first swing and reflexively punched him in the chest, not that the creature noticed. The dead man's expression remained blank and unreadable as he swung his fist at Zeb a second time. Attempting to block failed; the incoming attack hit him with the strength of a toppling pine, catapulting him off his feet and throwing him into the air. Zeb crashed into the side of a juniper trunk, bounced off, and hit the ground.

Driven by panic, he shoved himself to his feet before

he bothered to feel any pain—and found himself staring into the glowing eyes of a dead man who'd somehow managed to appear beside him in an instant.

The entity gave a low grunt and swung again.

Zeb ducked, scooting backward and gazing in shocked dismay at where the entity's fist knocked bark off a juniper tree. He scrambled to the side, muttering a steady stream of obscenities while trying to think of something he could do in order to stop a fiend with twice the strength of a plow horse. Bullets obviously wouldn't help. He hastily re-holstered both guns while evading a series of swings, the creature alternating left and right arms. It didn't punch at him as much as flail its arms in the walloping manner of clubs. No matter how fast he backed off, the creature kept up with him.

Squaring off against an insurmountable adversary he didn't understand would end in only one way. Running might seem cowardly, but in a situation like this, Zeb considered it wise. Before he could commit to a full on sprint, the creature abruptly reversed itself, swinging twice in a row with its right arm.

The unexpected change in rhythm caught Zeb unaware.

Cold knuckles crashed into the lower left side of his face. He thought the crunching sound coming from his jawbone meant something bad, but only had a fraction of a second to contemplate it before all went black.

Chapter Seventeen
Spirit Talker

Zeb stared up past the juniper branches at clear blue sky.

He realized he lay flat on his back upon bare earth, arms splayed out to either side. A short distance to his side lay the fallen tree Arnold had taken cover behind during their sorry excuse for a gunfight. Tingles and itching spread over the side of his head. The taste of blood filled his mouth. Much to his surprise, his guns remained loose in his grip.

That did not go well.

After a moment to adjust to being alive, he reached up to feel around his face. Everything seemed to be where it ought to be. Suffice to say, the creature had killed him with a single punch and The Lady saw fit to catch him at the gates of death yet again. A kink in his neck suggested that it had indeed been broken by the blow.

After a moment of lying there in silence, he sat up and blithely spent about fifteen minutes reloading both

Colts while sprawled on the ground like a small boy playing with toys.

"This right here is wasting time." He held up one gun. "These things ain't gonna be no good. Would help if you gave me *some* instruction. How am I supposed to stop that thing?"

A man's presence on his left made him sigh to himself. He waited a moment for Arnold to shoot him in the head. When no shot came, he decided to look in that direction. Rather than a bank robber, a Native American man stood there. The expression on his face said he had expected things to go about as they had.

"Don't suppose you're actually there," said Zeb. He reached out toward the spirit—and touched his arm. Upon finding the apparition not so much an apparition as a solid person, he raised both eyebrows.

"We are all here," replied the Native. "Can you truly say a spirit is less *here* than a man bound by flesh?"

Zeb rubbed his forehead. "It's too early for talk like that. Just woke up from the dead. Haven't even had a cup of Arbuckle's yet."

The shaman offered a placid smile.

After encountering a creature like he'd seen the previous night and coming back from the dead—again—the sight of a Native speaking perfect English shouldn't have shocked him as much as it did. Certainly, some of them had learned the language by now, but he expected they'd speak haltingly, with a strong accent.

Guess the rules change when you're a ghost. Bet he's speakin' whatever he speaks and I'm hearing it in English.

"You here to help?" asked Zeb.

"I am Keekuk, spirit talker of the Navajo Nation."

Zeb offered a hand. "Zebadiah Clemens. No fancy

title."

Keekuk regarded the outstretched hand as if unsure what to do with it.

"Pardon. Just somethin' white men do." Zeb lowered his arm.

"You are He Who Strides Between Worlds."

Zeb stuffed another paper cartridge into his second Colt, then pulled the ramming lever to stuff it into the chamber. "Something like that. Yeah. What was that thing?"

"Your people would call him a revenant."

Having never heard the term before, Zeb halfheartedly chuckled. "That don't help me. Ain't a clue what it means."

"He is dead but returned," said Keekuk.

"Well, so am I."

"In some ways, you and he are the same. In other ways, you are much different. Unlike you, a revenant *remains* dead, the soul trapped within a body that will not rest. Some of the man he used to be remains. His mind is fixated on something. The revenant has some ability to reason, but not as much as you or I."

"How much of a problem is this thing?" Zeb brushed dirt off his sleeves.

"My people sealed a great evil beneath the earth." Keekuk gestured to the west. "This fool set it loose. The darkness my ancestors sealed away has consumed him. Bullets will not kill what he has become."

"Yeah, I kinda figured that part out already." Zeb shoved his reloaded Colts into their holsters. "Any tips on what might stop him?"

"Dismembering with a sword or similar weapon, then burning the remains will delay it."

Zeb raised both eyebrows. "Delay? Not kill?"

"The revenant is already dead. If you destroy the body, you will succeed only in freeing the evil my ancestors tried to contain. It will take over another. You are not fighting the man you saw before you, but the darkness within him. It is the darkness you can neither see nor touch that must be defeated. The body is merely a tool, the way one might use a horse."

Zeb pushed himself upright. "Great. Sounds easy."

"I do not understand this about your people," said Keekuk. "Why do you say things when you mean the opposite?"

"It's called sarcasm." Zeb spat to the side. "Guess it's a way to cope with being frustrated."

Keekuk mulled this for a moment, then nodded. "All people have wisdom. Even the white man."

"Got any wisdom for me?"

"Yes." The shaman flashed a broad smile. "You are perhaps not the warrior I might have hoped for, but I sense you are capable of the task set before you. You will be best served by restoring the seal."

Zeb shook his head. "Ain't got the first clue what that means."

"Miles into the setting sun from where the white Lamb raises cows, you will find a canyon. Therein is a sacred cave." Keekuk gestured to the west. "My ancestors contained the dark spirit behind a symbolic door. Weak to a man but impassable to an entity such as what they battled. The prospector thought he had discovered hidden treasure and tore apart what he did not understand."

"Prospector?" asked Zeb.

Keekuk clasped his hands together in front of himself. "Morris Poole was his name in life. He sips from a cup of tainted blood with the Lamb."

God Almighty, can't any spirit ever speak in straight sense? Zeb squinted at him. "Just tell me what I'm supposed to do."

"Seek Wind Hawk's counsel. He will guide you on this path you must walk." Keekuk nodded once… and faded away.

"Well, I'll be." Zeb rubbed his forehead again. "I need to cut down on the dyin'. Startin' to make me see things."

He stared at the spot where the spirit had been. Unlike whiskey, dying probably wouldn't make him hallucinate or have a conversation with a tree mistaking it for a dead Native American shaman. Certain plants, if eaten, might do that to him, but simply dying and coming back?

Unfortunately, he doubted it. Which meant the conversation really happened.

Zeb groaned. Not only had he lost Arnold, he had to stop an ancient evil and didn't have the first idea how to go about fixing whatever 'seal' Keekuk spoke of or even where to find it.

Not knowing who or what a 'Wind Hawk' was, Zeb stood there for a while, thinking and making annoyed faces at the pronounced lack of Arnold Parrish, alive or dead. The man obviously took the opportunity of Zeb tangling with a supernatural fiend to make a run for it.

You're welcome, by the way. Ya good for nuthin' lousy…

Marshals and sheriffs had many stories of bizarre ways outlaws got lucky and avoided capture. He doubted any of them had a 'revenant' barge in on a gunfight.

Hell, maybe they had. This stuff seems to be real after all. 'Course, if it happened, ain't one of them willin' to speak of it.

Grumbling to himself, he stomped over to where his hat landed on the dirt and recovered it. As best he could tell, it had likely been about three hours before midnight when he found himself in an unwinnable brawl. The present color of the sky and position of the sun put the time at two or three hours before noon.

He'd been out for half a day.

Twelve hours. Plenty of time for Arnold to pick a direction and run. As much as Zeb did not want to admit it, he had nothing to go on. His pursuit of the bank robber would have to start all over again, and worse, he didn't know where to even begin. Had the good-for-nuthin' gone west to even wilder places? Could he have headed south for Mexico? North? It seemed unlikely the man would've chosen to travel east. The more established a place became, the greater the odds he'd be unable to evade the law.

A heavy growl came from his stomach.

Dying, apparently, was hungry work.

Zeb rubbed the back of his neck, which still ached from likely being broken, and wandered off in search of Jasper, calling out for the horse. The animal responded to his voice, showing himself after about twenty minutes —first with a hesitant peek around a tree, then seeming to trust the revenant had gone away, came trotting over as if nothing happened.

"Good to see you too, boy." Zeb patted Jasper on the neck, grateful to see the fiend hadn't hurt him. "Now, let's get out of these damn woods."

Chapter Eighteen
Cold Trail

Zeb leaned back in his chair at Hattie's, making the wood creak.

Though he'd only eaten one plate, he presently felt so full as to not be able to stand without assistance. Two other men ate their lunch at separate tables. One appeared to be some manner of salesman in a plum-colored suit and derby. The other man's cheap clothing and large frame said he'd likely come out here looking for work as a ranch hand. Men his size didn't often work in mines due to the cramped conditions. Zeb absent-mindedly compared him to Willie the Deserter. This man appeared roughly the same height but lanky, not even half the weight of the former soldier.

Thinking of Willie, Zeb shook his head. *That boy's a barrel with limbs.*

It occurred to him the spot of floor in the back of the room where he'd always seen the twins playing with their dolls was empty. An unsettling notion the children —and perhaps even Hattie—*had* died to the mysterious fever three years ago came out of nowhere. Perhaps this feeling stemmed from his conversation with the spirit, Keekuk, which had seemed little different in sense from talking to a living person. The girls' creepy staring, the way Hattie seemed to move like a phantom the other night, could she—or even this entire town—be on the other side?

The notion he might be sitting in an abandoned house talking with the spirit of its former owner stalled his thoughts.

Skin prickling, Zeb eyed the man in the plumb suit. Nothing about him seemed the least bit unusual… except for the color of his clothing. The prospective ranch worker also failed to give off the slightest trace of oddity.

Hattie entered the dining room area from the hallway leading deeper into the house, carrying a plate of food to the tall man. Seeing her again chased away his morbid worries. The woman looked perfectly normal and alive. Most likely, her daughters were too shy to play in a room with multiple strangers. The children had seemed to study him before deciding they didn't mind him. Perhaps they didn't trust just everyone.

Muttering to himself, Zeb stared into his water glass. Becoming aware of a greater reality than what most other people believed in seemed to be having an effect on him.

Dammit. Not everything is a ghost or monster.

"You all right, marshal?" asked Hattie after breezing over to his table. Though he couldn't see her feet thanks to a long navy blue dress, the sound of boot heels on the floorboards was an obvious contrast to the silent presence she'd been the previous night when he'd seen her in the hall.

"Not sure how to answer you there, ma'am." Zeb scratched idly at his stomach. "I've had better days and I've had worse days."

"Lost the man?" She leaned on the back of the empty chair facing him.

"Yep. Found him and he didn't have much interest in goin' quietly. We got to shootin' at each other and the noise attracted some manner of beast. By the time I chased it off, he'd skedaddled."

Hattie pursed her lips. "Well, that is certainly unnerving. What manner of beast did you see that required being chased off... or would *approach* a gunfight? Wouldn't animals run away from loud noises?"

"Usually." Zeb chuckled, then took a sip of water. "Don't rightly know what it was, other than big and hairy." He rubbed the back of his neck again. "And strong."

"Do you think it is a danger to us here?" Hattie pulled the chair she leaned on away from the table and sat.

Zeb mulled. "Don't hold me to this but, I'm goin' to say it's not too interested in the downtown here. Seems keen on the Lamb Ranch."

"Oh, those poor people." Hattie half-covered her mouth. "Any idea what it is? My sister-in-law, Annabelle, is convinced the Natives can turn normal animals into fierce monsters of war with some kind of magic."

He stared at her in a 'you don't seriously believe that' sort of way.

"Then again, Annabelle is a bit, how do you say... eccentric?" Hattie muffled a laugh. "I hadn't given her crazy worries much substance until just now when you say you ran into something big and hairy that shouldn't be there."

Zeb raised an eyebrow. "I didn't say it shouldn't be there."

"You did." Hattie leaned closer. "But not with words. I can tell. The face you made, the way you're sitting. You don't want to tell me the whole story for some reason."

He exhaled. "The name Morris Poole mean much to you?"

"I recall the man, yes." She nodded. "He stayed here a few days before leaving town after some manner of dispute with Calvin Lamb. Had to be on about two years ago by now."

"What happened?" Zeb continued rubbing his stomach, waiting for the food to settle.

Hattie excused herself for a moment. He waited patiently as she checked on the other two guests, then watched as she hurried off down the hall. Minutes later, she returned with a ewer of water and a glass for herself. After refilling his cup and pouring one for herself, she sat back down.

"The man worked for Mr. Lamb on the ranch," said Hattie. "By all accounts to reach my ears, there was nothing of particular note about him. They got into a dispute over wages. Morris believed he'd been shorted."

Zeb thought of the angry, undead fiend in the woods. Something wasn't adding up. "Shorted wages? That's all?"

Hattie sipped water. "I know Calvin Lamb about as well as a woman can know a man she's got no romantic interest in, and it wouldn't be like him to shortchange one of his workers. It would pain him to think someone thought that about him. If you ask me, Morris Poole confused himself. I'm sure it's just a misunderstanding."

Well, I'll be damned. How angry does a man have to

be to turn into a 'revenant' over a couple dollars?

The way Keekuk mentioned 'tainted blood' with the Lamb family, Zeb expected there had been some manner of messy romantic entanglement with Isabelle. A man catching one of his hired workers becoming too familiar with his wife would certainly lead to bad blood. If not that, then discovery of gold on the land or something much deeper and more significant than a disagreement over wages.

'Course, if a man ain't got all his marbles to begin with, might not take much at all to drive him crazy.

"Then again, that stuff happens all the time," said Hattie.

"What happens all the time?" Zeb picked up the ewer and refilled his cup.

"Ranch men arguing over wages." She waved dismissively. "They sign on and agree to one wage, then forget what it was by the time they get paid and think they were shorted. Or they claim to have done more than agreed to… it's common. The men try to take advantage where they can."

Zeb nodded. "Any idea what a Wind Hawk is?"

"Some kind of bird?" She chuckled. "And a fast one at that."

If not for being nose to nose with a walking dead man hours ago, Zeb might have laughed along with her. "Hmm. Maybe. Do you know of any Navajo in the area?"

Her demeanor shifted to caution. "I hear tell there may be some southwest, a day's ride past the creek."

"All right."

Eyes growing wider, Hattie leaned close, whispering, "Do you think they made whatever critter attacked you?"

"Not rightly, no." He shifted his jaw side to side. "If anything really is going on here that defies the reason of mankind's understanding, I do genuinely believe they tried to contain it. Seems that Poole fella broke something he shouldn't."

For a long moment, Hattie regarded him with a stare that could easily have called him insane as much as it gave off a sense of relief—as though she'd finally found someone else who believed in such things.

"Don't rule out someone trying to confuse you," whispered Hattie. "In fact, it could be my former husband making trouble for the Lambs. He's got to be furious that someone else is getting to enjoy the house *he* built. It wouldn't be in Edmund's nature to direct his anger toward innocent children and a wife, but no one knows how death can twist a man's mind around."

Zeb sat there in silence, looking at her. The woman truly believed her dead husband remained a restless— and dangerous—presence. Then again, her suggestion Edmund Cartwright was responsible for the misfortune plaguing the Lamb Ranch made more sense in a way. The man worked hard to build a home and ranch only to die relatively young to a mysterious illness. Not having the chance to enjoy the fruits of his labor would certainly motivate a spirit to cause harm far more so than an argument over wages.

However, Keekuk mentioned Morris Poole by name. If the revenant was, in fact, Edmund Cartwright, why would the spirit claim otherwise?

"Do you happen to have a picture of your husband about?" asked Zeb.

"In the attic." Hattie looked down. "I couldn't bear the sight of him staring at me. He seemed so angry."

Zeb rubbed his chin.

She looked up at him. "Why do you ask?"

"Small detail. No need to alarm yourself."

Her cheeks went corpse white. "You saw him, didn't you?"

Zeb raised both hands, trying to calm her. "No. Well... I don't believe I did. The big critter what interrupted my shootout with Parrish might not have been a proper animal."

"Wait here." She hurriedly got up and rushed out of the room.

"She's an odd one," called the salesman in the plumb suit. "Good luck with that."

Zeb glanced back at him, unsure how much the man heard. "Ain't tryin' to woo her, mister. She's a bit rattled at a ghost story, is all. You might want to keep an eye open when you sleep in this town. Better yet, don't sleep."

A nervous gurgle came from the salesman while the tall man continued smiling at his plate, not looking up at anyone, properly catching the gist of Zeb's words; that is, teasing the nervous city man.

Some minutes later, Hattie returned carrying a small picture frame wrapped in a handkerchief. Without a word, she rejoined Zeb at the table and offered him the bundle.

"Covered?"

"My mind plays too many tricks on me when I look at his face these days." She blushed. "Sometimes, I think they move. Especially when it is dark."

Zeb nearly whistled as he picked up the picture. He pulled the cloth back to reveal a silver-framed daguer-reotype of a man in his early twenties standing beside a noticeably younger Hattie seated in a wingback chair. Both seemed happy. Nothing whatsoever appeared sinister about the man. However, it struck him immediately that the revenant he'd run into could not possibly be Edmund Cartwright. Her former husband had a far more angular face than the square-jawed undead. The revenant, had he been alive, looked like the sort of man who would have adored living on his own in the woods hunting and fishing for survival. Edmund appeared wholly a product of the upper class. He'd not have lasted four hours in the woods alone.

I wouldn't either at that age. Guess I did learn something in the Army after all.

"It's an older photograph taken a few days after our wedding," said Hattie in a somber tone. "I was seventeen. He was twenty there. Feels like forever ago."

Zeb re-covered the picture and set it down on the table. "Not him. Whatever it was I saw didn't look the least bit like him."

"What did he look like?" asked Hattie, sounding like a young girl eager for a ghost story.

"About my height. Black hair. Squarest jaw I've ever seen. Short beard."

Hattie raised both eyebrows. "That does sound like Morris Poole. I wonder if that was him."

Zeb sighed at his empty plate. Since he no longer felt too full to move and had hopelessly lost Arnold Parrish's trail, he may as well do whatever he could to address the problem of an angry revenant. "Don't rightly know yet, ma'am, but I reckon I'm going to find out one way or the other."

"Be careful." She reached across the table and rested her hand on his wrist. "If you do happen to go to the ranch again, please tell Edmund that I didn't know he'd get sick. I was… just afraid of being so far away from town."

"Afraid? Or unwilling?"

Hattie fidgeted. "In truth, the land frightened me. It always felt as if something dark and sinister watched us from the west, in the mountains. I originally thought it might be the Natives, but… it was as if the land itself did not want to be lived on."

"Might not have been the land so much as whatever thing the Natives sealed away up in the hills."

"Well, whatever it was…" She fanned herself. "It took Edmund. I'm sure of it. If you go out there, you be careful."

"Will do." Zeb stood. "Thank ya again for the meal. One of the best I've had."

"You are welcome, marshal." She smiled.

Strangely, he almost asked for another hunk of bread despite having been stuffed only minutes before.

Yeah. Dyin's hungry work all right.

Chapter Nineteen
The Dead Can Wait

"Seek Wind Hawk's council..."

Zeb sighed. With little more to go on than a vague 'head northwest and look for Natives' rattling around in his head, he thanked Hattie for the food, room, and conversation before setting out down the hall. During the day, she left the door separating the guest rooms from the main house unlocked so anyone staying there could easily go to the dining room.

While he hadn't left anything in the bedroom he'd need, cutting through the house to the small stable behind it spared him having to walk all the way around the outside. He'd not yet made it halfway down the hallway when the door to the room beside the one he slept in two nights prior opened. Given the relatively narrow confines of the corridor, Zeb paused to give who-ever it was some room.

Arnold Parrish staggered out into view and crashed into the door opposite the one he came from.

The man appeared inebriated to the point he couldn't

stand properly without bracing himself against the wall. Zeb blinked in surprise. Of all the wild stories he'd ever heard regarding the crazy things to happen to lawmen chasing someone, spending the night in adjacent rooms beat all. Granted, Zeb hadn't exactly slept there last night, much less eight feet away from the man he tried to arrest.

He would have, if not for being briefly dead.

"What are the damn odds of that?" muttered Zeb.

At the sound of his voice, Arnold pushed himself away from the door he appeared to be in the process of kissing. What little color remained in his face disappeared as soon as he realized who he locked stares with.

At the sight of Zeb, Arnold attempted to scream, but managed only a repetitive wheezing.

The man reeked of cheap booze. He also had a look to him that reminded Zeb of the men on both sides of the Civil War who'd seen too much. One stood out in his mind: a rebel with bits of someone else's brain and skull spattered all over his chest. He'd evidently become disoriented and wandered to the wrong camp on the opposite side of the battlefield. Whether or not he deliberately intended to surrender or ended up in an enemy position due to confusion, Zeb couldn't say. Due to the man's stupefied silence and lack of aggression, the commander took it as an act of surrender and detained him as a prisoner of war.

Arnold had much the same demeanor. He did not seem interested in a fight. In fact, he stared at Zeb as if encountering the grim reaper himself. They said a bad enough fright could sober a man up in an instant, but Arnold still seemed likely to fall over if he tried to walk despite the seriousness on his face.

Debate raged in Zeb's thoughts. Given the inebriated

state of the man before him, it didn't seem likely he'd be much of a threat to anyone for a while. Even if he hadn't witnessed the revenant smash Zeb's head in and now saw a dead man back to arrest him, he'd still been grabbed and pulled face-to-face with a walking corpse. Some people would never be right again after either experience.

A not so small portion of Zeb's gut said he ought to forget about the bank robber and go take care of the thing only he could deal with. He weighed the possible harm the revenant might cause in the time it would take him to haul a bank robber to town and get him on a train with the odds of Arnold disappearing into the frontier never to be seen again.

Fate had, for reasons he couldn't fathom, thrown his quarry right back in front of him.

Perhaps not so much of a stretch after all. Harlon's Pass didn't have much of a main drag. If a man became too terrified to sleep without the protection of a locked door, this town offered only one option. Hattie did not serve liquor, nor did the town have a saloon. If Arnold possessed a stash of booze, it would've been at his campsite, but Zeb couldn't imagine the man had the nerve to go back to the forest where they encountered the revenant.

This meant he'd likely stolen the drink from a private home or maybe Branch's General Store.

One more count of petty thievery hardly mattered on top of everything else the man did, but it brought up the wonder if he'd shot anyone in the course of trying to steal a drink. That, in turn, made Zeb remember Rowena screaming.

Damn it all. The dead can wait.

"You know how this ends, right?" asked Zeb.

Arnold simply stared at him.

Zeb grabbed him by the shoulder. "Good. Glad you've come to see reason. No need for this to be unpleasant."

As if leading a partially alive mannequin along, Zeb guided the staggering outlaw out to the stables. Both stalls had an occupant: Jasper in one and an unknown horse in the other. Since the other animal still had a saddle and riding gear on it, Zeb assumed it to be Arnold's horse. He had no doubt been too out of sorts to take the time to unburden the animal.

After relieving Arnold of his guns, Zeb fished a set of manacles from his saddlebag and secured the thief's hands behind his back. That done, he hoisted the man up onto his horse. Arnold stared into the void, saying nothing nor moving at all while Zeb saddled Jasper, led the animal from the stall, and climbed up onto his back.

He took the reins of the second horse and led it—and Arnold—out of Harlon's Pass at an unhurried pace. No point rushing since it wouldn't be possible to make it all the way back to Silver Mesa in a single day. It would take galloping at full speed continuously for much longer than the animals could tolerate, and even then, the distance was too great to cover in one day.

Every so often while riding east, Zeb peered behind him, certain the spirit of Keekuk would be there, staring disapprovingly at him for leaving. He had his defense ready: if he let Arnold go, he'd be responsible for anyone else the man killed. Of course, taking time to attend to a bank robber by the same logic made him responsible for anyone the revenant might kill before his return. Zeb assuaged his doubts to that effect by dwelling on the fact he had no idea *how* to stop the creature.

But he was damn well going to figure out how.

The best he could think to do at the moment would be to get into another doomed fistfight and end up dead again. So, yes... he was going to need a better plan. What that plan might be.

I'll figure something out.

Remembering Rowena's indignant stare at being referred to as a child almost made him smile. At the ripe old age of thirteen, the girl certainly comported herself more like an adult than not. After the robbery, Zeb doubted Hilmer would send her to the bank again, even if the girl insisted she could handle it.

Arresting a murderer, child abductor, and bank robber he could do for certain. Speaking of which, stolen money likely still sat at the campsite. He ought to make a reasonable attempt to recover and return it.

He sighed, tugging on the reins, and reversed course toward the woods.

Doing so made Arnold finally snap out of his vacant staring. Most stories and legends of the West spoke of defiant outlaws marching to the gallows and mocking everyone around them, fearless of death. They seldom told of the far more common cases of men acting like terrified boys—some even begging for their lives in their last moments.

Zeb couldn't help but agree with the man's reasoning. Better to die in the heat of a gunfight than spend weeks sitting in a cell, going through a trial where everyone knew how it would end, then spending more days sitting in a cell awaiting one's inevitable demise. The fate sounded horrific. Merely thinking of it ought to be enough to scare any reasonable man away from committing the sort of crimes to put them in that situation. Alas, for whatever reason, the deterrent effect did not work as well as hoped.

To Zeb's surprise, Arnold neither begged, whimpered, nor even said a word as they re-entered the forest where the unexplainable encounter occurred. It took him until around noon to finally locate the spot. Arnold sat on his horse, silently watching as Zeb rummaged the campsite. He discovered three bank bags, still stuffed with cash, as well as some canned provisions, two more guns, paper cartridges, caps, and a shaving kit.

After packing the bulk of the materials in Jasper's saddlebags, Zeb tucked the shaving kit in the bag on Arnold's horse. That, he might still get some use out of before his inevitable date with a rope. A man ought to be cleaned up for his meeting with the hereafter.

Soon after he resumed riding east, Zeb got to thinking about the part he played in all of this. Did it make him something of a hypocrite to be spared the teeth of death only to serve as the agent of this man's demise? While he would not be killing the man directly, bringing him in accomplished the same end. Some might argue that once lawyers and judges got involved, Arnold's future didn't remain so set in stone. However, in Arnold's case, there had been over a dozen banks robbed, at least eight dead, and—as far as Zeb knew—one young girl kidnapped.

Whatever fate he's headed for is one of his own creation. Zeb gazed up at the clouds. *I am but an agent of the great machinery.*

He couldn't help but chuckle mentally. More so than ever, such a notion of being part of a cosmic process felt accurate. Everything that lives dies sooner or later. Natural process and all. He shifted his jaw side to side. This still applied to himself. He lived *and* died. The matter of his not *remaining* dead didn't necessarily break the rules.

As the hours of riding melted into each other, Zeb pondered his future. Whatever happened, be it remaining as he was for many decades or continuing to grow old as normal, he'd welcome it. The least he could do in return for the favor given him was to protect ordinary people from highly non-ordinary things.

Once the daylight started to show signs of weakening, Zeb decided to pick up the pace.

The sooner he got Arnold on a train, the sooner he could get back to Harlon's Pass.

Chapter Twenty
Seeing Things

Out in the middle of nowhere, Zeb stopped to rest for a few minutes and take care of some natural business. He removed the manacles from Arnold long enough for him to relieve himself and eat a can of beans.

The man still appeared to be not quite in the here and now, reacting a few seconds slower than normal and making no effort to escape. Sitting close while they ate allowed Zeb to notice numerous scratches on his face and rips in his shirt. He had no way to know what happened that night after the revenant killed him, but it certainly looked as though it at least chased Arnold through the woods.

It obviously hadn't caught him since he remained alive. Somehow, 'the Coyote' managed to elude the undead fiend. It might also be that he started running as soon as it went after Zeb and kept on running even though nothing followed him.

Once he decided they'd rested enough, Zeb re-manacled Arnold, heaved him up on the second horse, and resumed riding for Rawhide.

A few minutes after they got underway, Arnold finally broke his silence.

"What was that thing, marshal?"

Zeb pondered how to answer. It likely wouldn't make too much difference what he told the man since Arnold would undoubtedly end up swinging from a rope in a few months. Being truthful might get him talking in a way that caused others to think him insane. Depending on the judge involved, it could work for or against him. Some courts might hasten the execution of an insane, dangerous man, while others might show mercy and commit him to a long prison stay instead of death.

"A dead man who ain't got enough sense to stay sleepin'," said Zeb. "Don't rightly know the details. Some manner of bad blood with one of the families out there."

"What's it want?"

Zeb shrugged. "Reckon it's like an angry drunk. Got somethin' stuck in its craw and lacks the reason to understand it... so just gets violent with whoever happens to be close enough to reach."

About ten minutes passed in silence before Arnold blurted, "I saw it break your neck."

"You saw wrong, obviously." Zeb rubbed the back of his neck. "If it did that, I wouldn't be here."

"The crack was so damn loud, I *felt* your neck break. It echoed in my bones." Arnold shuddered. "Looked like half your face flew off."

"You were rattled," said Zeb, calm as anything. "Scared. Seeing things. I'm here, ain't I?"

Arnold exhaled hard. "We really saw that thing? Or did I imagine that, too?"

"Well... either we both let our imagination run wild

and imagined the same thing, but more likely we ran into some cursed ol' prospector."

"A prospector," mumbled Arnold.

Zeb patted Jasper on the neck and whispered, "Almost there, boy. Just take us a little farther and you'll get somethin' good to eat."

"How's a damn prospector end up like that?" asked Arnold in a wavering voice.

The sky ahead of them in the east had darkened to indigo. Straight above, it remained a rich blue while far behind them to the west, it remained sunny. Zeb felt as though he existed on the literal border between night and day. The shadowy apparitions of cacti around them became a congregation of silent judgment. In that fleeting moment, reality seemed as though he approached the border of Hades with the realm of the living behind him and the departed up ahead. Like him, the cactus-silhouettes dwelled in neither place.

"They say dark deeds always come back eventually, one way or the other." Zeb squinted into the dark, searching for any trace of Rawhide. "Preachers talk about Hell, an' we think of it as some other place. The longer I live, the more I think for some poor bastards, Hell is right here."

Again, Arnold shivered. "Am I gonna end up like that thing?"

"No idea." Zeb shrugged. "Ain't my choice to make."

After a long pause, Arnold whispered, "What are you?"

"A marshal."

"Come on now." Arnold attempted to wipe his nose on his shoulder, making the manacles behind his back clatter. "You saw that thing, too, and here you's actin' like it ain't no big deal. Damn thing bashed your face in and here you are. Am I dead already? Are you Death come to take me?"

Zeb shrugged. "In a way, yes. But you ain't dead yet."

A cluster of weak lights appeared in the distance—lanterns inside windows and street lamps.

"There it is," muttered Zeb. "Rawhide."

"W-what are you gonna do with me?"

"Same thing any busy marshal would. Stick you on a train to El Paso to stand trial."

Arnold took a deep breath. "You really came after me just on account of that kid?"

"Not entirely. I came after you on account o' you killin' people and robbin' banks. What you did to that girl just lit a fire. After that, I'd have followed ya all the way to California and back."

"I didn't try to kill her. Figure she'd grab the branch."

"Don't matter none to me what you thought. What if she didn't get a hold of it? If I hadn't been *right* there, she'd have fallen. The blasted root tore outta the rock. She got damn lucky."

"If you hadn't been right there, I wouldn't have tossed her over the side."

Zeb glared at him until the urge to break his jaw passed. "What would you have done with her if I hadn't been on your heels?"

The thief shrugged. "Not rightly sure, marshal. Didn't really think much about it. Prolly set her loose once we got ta Rawhide."

"And have her run straight to the sheriff?"

Arnold fidgeted. "All right, maybe let her go somewhere she couldn't get to the law so fast."

"And have her get lost, starve, maybe eaten by coyotes or whatever. You'd leave a young girl her age alone out in the middle of nowhere? That's almost more cruel than throwin' her to her death. Least that would'a been quick."

Arnold kept quiet for a moment. "Weren't nothin' personal. Kid just happened to be there."

"Figured. Don't change the wrongness of it."

The outlaw kept his mouth shut for some time. Right as the buildings of Rawhide came into view out of the night, he whispered, "Just get it over with already. Shoot me here and be done with it."

"Nawp," said Zeb. "What happens to ya now ain't my choice ta make."

Chapter Twenty-one
Home... Almost

Zeb tried not to get too comfortable sitting behind his desk.

He only intended to stay in town for as long as it took to put Arnold Parrish on a train to El Paso. Initially, he'd taken Arnold to Rawhide hoping to save some time, but the train schedule proved uncooperative. Faced with a choice of leaving the bank robber in a cell for eleven days until the next train arrived or spending a day and a half riding back to Silver Mesa—where the trains showed up more frequently—he decided to do the opposite of sitting around.

Of course, he could have left Arnold in custody at Rawhide and gone back to look into the revenant situation... but couldn't come up with a reasonable explanation to give the local sheriff for it. He also didn't expect his prisoner would remain in such a state of shock for too much longer. An almost two-week period of sitting in a cell would likely give him the opportunity to collect his wits and formulate a plan of escape. So, Zeb had gone right from the train station to the trail once he learned how long it would take, not bothering to even stop in at the sheriff's office in Rawhide.

Despite the extra two days of travel, the return to Silver Mesa felt like the safest choice.

At least the weather had been cooperative. The unusual heat wave passed. Though it remained hotter than he found pleasant, the temperature no longer made everyone miserable. Two nights out in the wilds forcing himself to lurk at the bare edge of sleep so he could react in case Arnold made a move all but demanded he put off plans to return to Harlon's Pass for another day. He hadn't fared well against the revenant while mostly rested. Taking on such a creature while in a sleep-deprived delirium wouldn't make things any better for him.

He busied himself writing two documents. The first was a telegraph to be sent ahead of the prisoner to El Paso, alerting the Marshal's Service there of Arnold's imminent arrival. Once he finished that, he wrote out the official 'investigation report' of the events at the bank, detailing the robbery, the death of Amos Dumont age twenty-one, plus the kidnapping—and attempted murder—of Rowena Paine, age thirteen. According to his official explanation of events, he'd tracked Harry McDonald down and taken him in with minimal difficulty. Upon locating Arnold Parrish hiding out in the woods near Harlon's Pass, a gunfight ensued which had the unfortunate circumstance of being interrupted by an unknown wild animal.

Not that it would make a significant difference in Arnold's fate before a judge, but initiating a gunfight with a US Marshal did qualify as another count of attempted murder.

Sheriff Ervin had recovered enough from being shot to be off bed rest. His still-healing injury prevented him from doing anything more demanding than paperwork. Zeb declined to tease him about this not being much different than normal. After all, the man *had* gone running toward a shootout with no hesitation.

He's not as lazy as he looks… as long as he don't have ta leave town.

"Impressive ya got the sumbitch," said Ervin.

"Figured he would. Just not this fast." Jim Carberry spat into the little brass pail beside his desk.

Zeb finished folding his report and tucked it into an envelope for the trip. "Got lucky, is all. That and didn't give 'em much time to go far."

"How'd you manage it?" asked Conley.

A low grumble of discontent echoed across Zeb's mind. He kept it to himself, remaining silent and stoic on the outside. Talk of wanting to rush right back out to Harlon's Pass to investigate something not one of these men would take seriously wouldn't be received well. He half thought of a more plausible excuse involving possibly suspicious circumstances surrounding the death of Edmund Cartwright, but didn't manage to solidify it enough before the pending silence grew too awkward to continue trying to think of something.

Zeb explained the rudiments of his pursuit, leaving out the supernatural details after his gunfight with Arnold.

"Sounds crazy." Conley whistled. "Shootin' at each other in the dark like that."

"Ehh, more like we shot random trees while cracking wise at each other." Zeb laughed. "Neither one of us hit anything but wood. Damn shame I ran myself outta bullets before that critter showed up."

"Ain't no bears out this way," said Ervin. "What manner of critter was it?"

"Don't know." Zeb scratched his eyebrow. "Too dark to get a good look at it, and it ran off just as fast as it came charging at us. Maybe a bison or some such thing."

A brief discussion on the exact nature of the creature shifted to Zeb announcing the plan to take Arnold to El Paso by train tomorrow. He'd have preferred requesting another marshal come out here to handle the escort, but doing so would open the door to a bunch of questions he couldn't really answer. And answering with 'heading back out to Harlon's Pass to hunt the undead' wouldn't go over so well. If his boss, Beecher McNett, got wind of that, Zeb might soon find himself an ordinary citizen again.

Sitting at his desk instead of being on the way back to Harlon's Pass cinched an urgent knot in his guts bad enough without the added delay of a round-trip train ride to El Paso.

Least I don't gotta drag him to San Antonio.

"Somethin' ain't right with that man," said Conley, while peering down the hall toward the holding cells.

"Obviously." Ervin shook his head. "A man who's right in the head don't rob banks."

Conley faced his boss. "That's not what I meant, sheriff. He's addled somehow."

"Addled how?"

"Like he ain't all there."

Ervin grumbled something inaudible.

The front door flew open. Laura barged in and rushed over to Zeb. "By the grace of…"

Zeb managed to get to his feet before she collided with him. "What's gone and upset you now?"

Evidently unconcerned with the other men watching, she embraced him firmly for a moment before leaning back to make eye contact. She seemed a bit pale, with a mild bit of redness around her eyes. He didn't think she'd been weeping, merely close to it.

"I can't rightly explain." She exhaled in relief. "Just got all kinds of worried about you for no reason, like something bad happened."

A pulse of ache throbbed in Zeb's neck. "I'm fine. Just dealin' with a bank robber who didn't want to be taken in."

Laura ran her fingers through her hair. "Sorry. It's just that... I was startled awake right as I fell asleep the other night. An overwhelming sense of dread came over me. I haven't had a feeling like that since..." Laura looked down. "Suppose my emotions got the better of me."

"Naw, your intuition's good." Zeb attempted to say 'I'll explain later' with a stare. Had he been in private with her somewhere out of earshot of anyone else, he might've admitted the truth. Somehow, she really had sensed the moment he'd been killed. He didn't fancy deceiving her, but for the same reason he needed to escort Arnold himself, he couldn't speak openly of certain things in front of too many people. "The damn fool in back started shootin' at me."

Laura squeezed his hand. "It seems that I am predisposed to worrying of history repeating. I'm glad you're back home, safe."

"About that..." Zeb exhaled.

Though her eyes widened in apprehension, the rest of her face gave off annoyance or anger.

"There's somethin' I still need ta do over by Harlon's Pass once I get this bank thing sorted."

Laura hardened her stare.

"Ol' Zeb's fixin' ta get divorced afore he ever gets married." Ervin started to laugh, but grabbed his side, wincing. "Gah. Dammit."

Zeb grumbled to himself, then took Laura's hand. She took the hint and followed him outside.

***

They ducked around the corner of the sheriff's office, hoping the narrow gap between it and the dry goods store offered sufficient privacy for a conversation of an unusual nature.

"I do hope you are planning to share whatever it was you chose not to say in front of the other men." Laura folded her arms.

He stared into her eyes for a long few minutes, searching for the courage to tell her what really happened. While he didn't feel as if he'd done anything reckless—given he couldn't die—her fear and worry had been genuine enough to make him feel responsible for her feelings. Admitting the truth to her, crazy as it was, would either prevent such a panic in the future... or completely ruin any possible future they may share.

If she thought him crazed, she'd likely not spare another word to him. Of course, if she believed him... a woman who'd already lost a husband might spring at the chance to spend her life with a man who couldn't lose his own. However, for it to provide her comfort, she'd have to believe it. Alas, Zeb did not want to prove his claims. The sight of him dying right in front of her and coming back might do permanent damage to her mind. It would be one thing if bad luck caused it by chance. But to shoot himself with her watching simply as a demonstration crossed all manner of lines.

Besides, The Lady might not take too kindly to such a thing. It would be just his luck she objected to the spectacle of it and picked that death to let him stay on the other side.

Another problem arose in the way Arnold Parrish reacted to seeing Zeb come back from the dead. In the lawman's opinion, very few people could see proof of the supernatural world and remain the same. Even if Laura believed him and accepted it, he worried about the effect being made aware of the 'greater reality of existence' would have on her—and on Heath. He couldn't, in good conscience, force such a drastic change in their lives.

At least… not yet.

I will have to tell her everything before a preacher seals the deal… if'n we take things so far.

As sure as he now felt circumstances sent him to Harlon's Pass intentionally, he didn't know how to tell Laura about it. For that matter, he worried The Lady would be upset with him for putting his mundane responsibilities as a marshal ahead of his cosmic ones. Instinctively, he raised the defense of being thrown into a situation with no information. The least The Lady could do would be to tell him *how* to take on whatever entity she decided he needed to address. Sighing, Zeb conceded the information he lacked had, in fact, been offered to him by a ghost. He merely needed to go after it.

"There's a situation down there I need to look into, and it ain't exactly one I can put in the books."

She raised both eyebrows.

"There's a widow there who's got it in her mind that her dead husband's angry spirit is after her and a couple o' little ones." Zeb's eye twitched in response to the half-truth. "Reckon it's someone still alive pesterin' her. Can't rightly go tellin' the boys I'm off on a ghost hunt."

"Another widow?" Laura let her arms fall slack.

"It ain't like that." He gently grasped her above both elbows, looking into her eyes. "Ain't but one lady in the West who's on my mind all the time."

She smiled.

"B'sides. That one ain't got no interest in findin' another man. She's convinced the ghost of her dead husband would violently object."

"Oh." Laura bit her lower lip. "Do you think such things can happen?"

"Well, at risk of sounding a bit addled myself, I will say my opinions on the subject have changed over the past six months or thereabout." Zeb paused. "I would no longer immediately discount such a claim as nonsense."

"Would you think less of me if I said I thought I saw... him?"

"Him?"

Laura fidgeted. "My dead husband."

Zeb raised both eyebrows. "I would not think less of you, but I would ask when and what happened."

"Few weeks back. I might have simply been dreaming." Laura's cheeks tinted blush. "Twas real soon before sunrise one morning and I could've sworn he was standing there beside my bed. Gave me this single nod and a smile. I... confess to maybe having been dreaming of a certain marshal right before waking."

"Oh?" Zeb couldn't help but smile.

She held her chin up, the blush deepening. "Call me crazy, but it seemed as though he wanted me to be happy and safe, even approved of you."

Zeb brushed a hand across her hot cheek. "If you see

him again, you tell him I'll do everything in my power to make sure you are both happy and safe."

"That does not include gallivanting around the desert."

Zeb chuckled. "It's only gallivanting when there's a self-aggrandizing purpose behind it. I need to get Parrish to El Paso in one piece, then head back on down to Harlon's Pass."

"The widow…" Her expression fell in disappointment.

"That's part of it." Zeb glanced around to ensure their privacy, then lowered his voice. "Wasn't sure what sort of reaction you'd have to hearin' talk of ghosts, but there's more to the story."

Laura lifted her gaze off the road to stare at him. "Figured as much. At risk of you thinking me bereft of my senses, I have seen some things throughout my life I dare not speak of to most people. Sometimes, I almost wonder if I'm drawn to spirits."

Irony nearly made Zeb laugh. "All right. There's a man down there with a vendetta of sorts against an entire family. Tricky part is, I ain't sure if he's still fully among the living."

Her face paled.

"It's nothing to worry about." Zeb winked. "The man don't even have guns. Just a nasty right hook."

She sighed at him. "Think about what it would do to me—and my son—if anything happened to you."

"I do think about that." Zeb grasped her hand. "Every day. I ain't about to do nothin' stupid. But, what kind'a man would I be givin' my word to a woman with two kids half Heath's age that I'd make sure she weren't in no danger an' not goin' back there ta do it."

Laura rested her head against his shoulder. "I understand it, but that doesn't mean I have to like it." After a moment, she lifted her head and kissed him. "Maybe I do like it more than I care to admit. Speaks to the kind of man you are."

"Just doin' what I feel's right. But first I leave ta El Paso tomorrow."

"Well then, I may insist you spend what remains of this day in my company."

He grinned. "Much obliged to."

Chapter Twenty-two
Restless

An afternoon and evening spent with Laura did much to take Zeb's mind away from his worries.

Even if they'd spent most of the daylight talking while tending to her home—her cleaning while he moved a few things too heavy for her—and watching after the boy, he found it as pleasant as an idle day in the countryside. Heath asked for a story about hunting the bank robber, a request he happily indulged.

The strangeness began soon after sunset.

Zeb stood in the doorway to the little bedroom where Heath patiently waited for his mother to fetch him a cup of water. The squeak of the well pump out back preceded a startled gasp. Sensing alarm in her voice, he started toward the door but stopped as she dashed inside, seeming pale.

"Zeb?" whispered Laura.

He hurried over to her. "What's given you a fright?"

"Not a fright as much as a start." She nodded toward the door. "Do you see anything odd out there?"

Zeb approached the back door and peeked out. About ten paces past the well stood an oddly pallid man wearing a nice suit and derby. The most peculiar thing about him might have been that he resembled a photograph—being entirely devoid of hue—if not for the clearly fatal gunshot wound gaping in his forehead.

Certain he observed a spiritual apparition, Zeb regarded the man for a moment in silence. The spirit seemed neither frightful nor perturbed, merely… expectant, as if he waited for something. After a moment of contemplation, Zeb mumbled, "Arnold Parrish do that to you?"

The specter nodded once.

"My condolences." Zeb bowed his head at the man before backing into the house and facing Laura. "Reckon he's one of the victims of the man I'm takin' to El Paso in the morning."

Laura glanced down at the cup of water in her shaking hand until she managed to stop trembling. "Is he…?"

"Yes."

"Why is he here?"

"I'd only be guessing. Don't have no way to know for sure," said Zeb.

"Guess then." She took a few deep breaths.

"He's come to watch the man who killed him face trial." Zeb shrugged. "Might mean they're gonna hang Parrish soonish."

Laura started down the hall to bring Heath his water. "I don't know whether to be comforted or frightened at the thought of his victims waiting for him on the other side."

Zeb followed her. "Only one who should be frightened is him."

"Yes." Laura gave him a 'let's stop talking about this in front of the boy' stare, then went into the bedroom.

***

Oddities continued throughout the night.

Zeb counted four other spirits who appeared at random, watching them. Since he had not married Laura, he didn't anticipate anything would happen of an improper nature between them that night, even if there hadn't constantly been visitors showing up in the house. They talked about various subjects unrelated to spirits and death. Prior to making her way out west, she'd been fascinated by the arts and education. She'd unofficially obtained copies of various books and dabbled with subjects taught in universities not open to women. While she couldn't put it to any practical use to support herself, Laura possessed a rather surprising repertoire of knowledge involving the sciences and literature.

In truth, Zeb hadn't read much since he ended up in the Union Army, but he had done so enough in his younger years to spend a few hours talking about Shakespeare and Voltaire with her. Never in his life had time flown by so quickly, even if she possessed a much deeper knowledge of literature.

Being proper and all, he returned home to sleep, spotting two different spirits watching him. With each new apparition to reveal itself to him, his uneasiness grew. The way the deceased victims stared took on a sterner meaning. As it seemed neither hostile nor a warning, he assumed the spirits had come to make sure he didn't have a last minute change of mind and leave the Parrish matter unfinished.

The last spirit to catch his eye, a woman old enough to be his mother, appeared briefly right inside the door of his house when he opened it. Her sudden presence almost startled him back onto his posterior.

"All right. All right. I get the message," he rasped. "El Paso it is."

She vanished.

***

The next morning, Zeb woke a few minutes before sunrise.

He hurried a breakfast of bread and jam, then made his way to The Silver Cup for coffee. After downing two mugs as fast as he could drink them, he went to the sheriff's office to rouse Arnold. Conley Meade, being young and dutiful, had arrived at the jailhouse before him and already manned his desk.

"Mornin'," said the young deputy when Zeb walked in.

"Mornin' to you." He tipped his hat.

Conley stood. "You fancy a helping hand? Man like what you got back there knows he's goin' to hang, might try something. Be less inclined to do that if there's two of us."

"If you want. But will Ervin get his skivvies in a knot over you leaving?"

"Nah. It's what, two hours each way? We'll be back by evenin'."

"Something like that." Zeb nodded. "Appreciate it."

The two men headed down the hall toward the holding cells where the only occupant—Arnold Parrish —remained asleep. Evidently still rattled into a near catatonic state, the bank robber barely reacted to being dragged out of bed, escorted to the bathroom, then secured in manacles and leg irons.

Strangeness continued on the train platform.

Stares from dead people bored into Zeb from all directions. Some spirits he saw, others, he only sensed their eyes upon him. Arnold mostly gazed into space or at the ground. A handful of men and women who either waited for the train or had come to greet people arriving on it regarded the man with curiosity often reserved for zoo animals or circus freaks.

Zeb ignored the whispers of the living going on around them. The events at the bank being so fresh in everyone's mind, it didn't take long for the small crowd waiting for the train to deduce the prisoner had something to do with it. Whenever anyone approached to ask what he'd done, Zeb matter-of-factly informed them he was one of the men who robbed Josiah Bullinger and presently on his way to face a judge in El Paso.

A few people questioned why the judge here couldn't hear the case.

Being told Arnold had robbed multiple banks in multiple places and killed haphazardly along the way, so a trial would need to properly address *all* his crimes, not only the one in Silver Mesa, seemed to calm the growing discontent. The other thing playing on Zeb's mind that he didn't say involved deferring any revenge away from his home town. He hadn't discovered anything to suggest Arnold Parrish had friends or family who'd take umbrage at his imminent hanging and come after the judge. However, if such parties existed, better they don't cause trouble here.

Not long after full daylight, the train arrived in a bustle of steam, howling whistles, and the screech of steel on steel. People disembarking for Silver Mesa gave

Arnold curious and wary glances before hurrying away. Conley alternated between seeming like a taller version of Heath—a boy completely thrilled to be 'playing marshal'—and a vigilant deputy. Being relatively young, the fellow still had an idealistic view of the law and believed in the inherent nobility of upholding it.

He hasn't seen enough of the world to understand how truly awful some men can be. Zeb shook his head then tugged on Arnold's arm, pulling him up the steps to the train car. *Here's hoping he never does.*

Zeb directed Conley to sit closest to the window, put their prisoner between them, and sat on the aisle. Rows of none-too-comfortable wooden seats—little different from cheap dining room chairs bolted to the floor—promised a lengthy ordeal. The dull green velvet pads pretending to be cushions released a pungent years' old aroma of varnish and pipe tobacco baked into the wood by many days under a desert sun.

Fortunately, with the windows open, the passenger car did not become overly stifling. He hoped it would cool off once they got moving.

About twenty minutes after boarding, the conductor came by to check tickets. Soon after that, the train pulled out of the station, heading south for El Paso. Word was the newer generation of steam locomotives could travel at speeds approaching sixty miles per hour. This explained the diminishing frequency of train robberies. Horses simply couldn't catch up to them anymore unless the bandits obstructed the tracks in a way that forced the train to stop.

An hour into the ride, Zeb felt watched. Sure enough, he lifted his gaze to make eye contact with the same man in fancy duds who'd appeared by Laura's water pump. A shaft of dusty sunlight coming in the window illuminated the green velvet behind his chest. During the day, the apparition did not appear even remotely solid, in fact, he teetered at the bare edge of visibility. Another seat three rows behind him and to the left contained a transparent woman who seemed about thirty years of age. She glared at Arnold. Signs of a bullet wound in the side of her head suggested she had been an innocent bystander rather than a deliberate target.

Here and there, empty seats in the train car gradually filled with specters over the course of the next two hours. No one other than Zeb reacted to their presence. Whenever a live person seated next to a ghost moved too much, the spirit dissipated into a fog. By the time the train pulled into the station at El Paso, Zeb counted no fewer than twenty-two individuals, all but three of them men. Based on their attire, most seemed to have been bankers and deputies.

"You've been busy," muttered Zeb.

Arnold didn't respond.

"They're all here... the dead." Zeb eyed him. "Do you see them, too?"

Arnold glanced at him. "Stop tryin' to mess with my head."

Zeb considered describing some of the ghosts in case the man recognized them, but decided against it. "You don't have to take my word. Fair bet you'll see them soon enough."

Arnold shuddered.

The spirits all vanished at the same time when the passengers rose to their feet to get off. With their disappearance, the heavy mood lifted. As much as he wanted to hurry back to Harlon's Pass, Zeb felt better about his decision to bring in Arnold Parrish himself.

However, a heaviness in the pit of his gut urged him to be quick about it. He dreaded returning to the Lamb Ranch only to find everyone there dead.

Nothing to gain by worryin' at this point.

Zeb stood, pulled Arnold to his feet, and guided him down the aisle to the door.

Once out of the train, Zeb grasped the man's right arm while Conley stood on the other side holding his left. Together, they walked their prisoner down the street. Conveniently, the train station sat on the main thoroughfare in town, only six or seven blocks from the building serving as the US Marshal's Service office, jailhouse, and court.

For the most part, Conley resisted the temptation to gawk around at the big city and kept his attention focused on the bank robber. His ability to put duty above personal curiosity both surprised and impressed Zeb. The young man would have plenty of time to sightsee after they dropped their prisoner off.

Being in El Paso almost made Zeb miss where he'd grown up back East. The street here had more people walking about in direct sight than lived in all of Silver Mesa. He'd once enjoyed living among such large crowds. Time spent in the army among men he had little in common with beyond the notion the traitors needed to be contained acclimated him to the peace of being alone.

The apparitions continued to appear at random among the citizens. Neither Arnold, Conley, nor anyone else still among the living paid them any notice. Only Zeb seemed to see them. Each spirit popped up briefly before fading away. Some walked among the people, passing close by. Others manifested at a distance, staring from alleys or even windows of nearby stores. Their presence did not unsettle Zeb *too* much as their eerie stares fixated on the man who killed them.

Arnold's complete passivity and utter lack of any attempt to escape did surprise him. Few outlaws went quietly to their fate when it all but seemed assured they would end up dangling on a rope. Whatever he'd seen in the woods a few days ago might have driven him to take his own life at some point had Zeb not stumbled into him. Perhaps he considered this an easier way out. Zeb thought back to Arnold's comment about the fate of evil men. It could be that the outlaw hoped by surrendering to justice he might be spared from ending up as a revenant—or some other horrid monster.

It took a little more than an hour at the Marshal's Office to check the prisoner in, turn over his report, and have a brief conversation with Beecher McNett about the situation. Since it had been almost a year from the last time Zeb visited El Paso, the marshal decided to catch up with him about the goings on. The man had gone prematurely grey, his hair almost white, and wore it in an overly neatly styled manner complete with a scrap of a cottony mustache resembling a fuzzy caterpillar asleep on his upper lip. He spoke in a lilting southern drawl, as if measuring every word to fit neatly into the rhythm of his cadence—or thinking over his sentences twice lest he say something potentially troublesome from a political sense.

I've never met a man who could say so little in so many words.

Zeb contained his restlessness as much as humanly possible while wishing the meeting would hurry up. It bothered him to be sitting around jaw jacking when an innocent family had an abomination stalking them.

At long last—some fifty minutes later—Beecher appeared to realize he had a whole host of other things he needed to do (likely more hand shaking and seeking campaign donations) and thus stood to offer a hand.

"Keep up the good work out there, Zebadiah."

"Sure thing, Marshal McNett." Zeb shook hands. "I'm just dyin' to get back out there."

Beecher chuckled. "Well, don't take that too literal like. We need all the good men we can keep."

Happy to be free, Zeb wasted no time leaving the building after collecting Conley from the hallway outside the marshal's office.

Not a single odd spirit appeared for the remainder of the time they spent having lunch and waiting for the next train home.

Chapter Twenty-three
Three Graves and a Lost Lamb

Zeb almost rushed straight from the train station to the stable to grab Jasper and begin the trip to Harlon's Pass. The horse seemed to sense the urgency in him and proceeded at a pace somewhat faster than walking but not quite a trot.

Each minute since he'd completed his responsibility with Arnold seemed to worsen the sense he'd chosen poorly. Perhaps what's done was done, and it would be too late to spare the Lamb family an unfortunate demise.

Did sacrificing a family of innocents to their fate outweigh the need to bring a man like Arnold Parrish to justice? If he knew for a fact that doing so would result in the family being killed, he'd not have thought twice about abandoning his hunt for Arnold. While anyone else the man shot before being apprehended would have weighed on Zeb's conscience, the deaths of bankers or lawmen would not have burdened him as heavily as those of an innocent family.

Did this revenant have enough of a soul left to spare

an innocent like Ada who had nothing to do with his wages, or might he go after her first to torment her father?

Going through Rawhide would make travel easier due to the more established route and known terrain. Even if he had the supernatural sense of direction to go in a perfectly straight line from Silver Mesa to Harlon's Pass, he'd still end up having to sleep one night out in the wilds. It wouldn't do anyone any good if he forced himself to ride without stopping and arrived as a barely functional half-person.

Spending the night at a hotel didn't make it any easier to sleep, but it did spare him the time and effort of cooking for himself.

Two days and some hours after depositing Arnold Parrish at the Marshal's Office in El Paso, Zeb returned to Harlon's Pass to find an unusually large number of people congregating in the street. One end of the crowd appeared to gravitate toward the church while the other collected outside Branch's General Store. This momentarily perplexed Zeb until he recalled something about Mr. Branch being the closest thing they had to a mayor.

He approached the group of people abuzz with conversation about how 'something had to be done.'

"Pardon," said Zeb to a middle-aged, slightly overweight man who had a look of certainty about him. "What's going on?"

Everyone in conversational distance stopped talking and looked at him. An auburn-haired woman in her mid-twenties scowled at him as if he'd done something wrong. The not-yet-one-year-old baby she held seemed a bit bewildered.

The older man he'd initially addressed shook his head in a somber manner. "Death at the Lamb Ranch."

"And another on the road," added the younger man beside him.

The ranch… Coldness raked at Zeb's guts. "Damn…"

"You get that sumbitch you were after?" snapped the woman.

Zeb understood the implication. He tipped his hat to her. "Ma'am, the feller I'd been trackin' has been caught. In fact, he's in El Paso as we speak to stand trial. Whatever happened here, he didn't do it."

This seemed to satisfy her and most of the others.

Meanwhile, the large man gestured to the west. "Couple o' ranch hands turned up dead. An' the little daughter's gone missing. Half the town's out that way now searchin' the land for her."

All of a sudden, it made sense to Zeb why the people here all appeared either on the older side except for a few young mothers who couldn't leave their babies alone. Everyone capable of doing so had run off into the countryside to help look for Ada.

At no point prior in Zebadiah Clemens' life had he felt so simultaneously relieved and troubled. Two ranch hands had been killed—not the entire family. *Missing* didn't necessarily mean tragedy, yet evil often preyed on the most innocent. If anything happened to Ada Lamb, no amount of rationalizing would lift the guilt off his soul.

Any marshal or lawman could've chased Parrish. None of them could deal with a revenant. Hell, he hadn't yet convinced himself *he* could deal with the revenant, but knew he had *some* chance of success where others had none. As of now, the only thing he knew for certain was not to use bullets on it. Keekuk's ghost advised a sword and or fire. Shy of going back to an old Union

165

Army base and trying to talk someone into selling him a cavalry saber, he didn't rightly know where on Earth to get a sword.

He *did* know that sitting there thinking wasn't helping.

"Three men," said the annoyed woman. "Two ranch hands over at Lamb's and another poor bastard they found on the path east toward Rawhide."

"Figure that fella was on his way here," said a third man while bowing his head. "What kinda damn fool travels through the night like that?"

The older, portly man coughed. "The deceased all had their heads mashed in."

Zeb nodded at them. "Much obliged for the information. I'll head out to the ranch and help with the search as best I can."

"Family'd appreciate that." The man waved to him before resuming his debate with the others around him as to whether it would be more helpful to seek aid from the pastor or demand 'Mayor Branch' do something.

The auburn-haired woman eyed Zeb suspiciously. She might be simply thinking he wouldn't be of any use here, but he couldn't help but feel the accusation in her eyes as if she knew. Three men—and possibly a child— died because he'd chosen to drag a bank robber back to jail.

Shouting from the church end of town drew his attention to Curtis Small. The man blamed 'the damned savages' for both taking the little girl and killing all three men. He appeared to be trying to rile up enough of the older men still there to go with him and 'take her back by force.' That he was both young and able-bodied enough to be out searching for Ada, yet chose to remain here trying to get a mob to go kill Natives spoke volumes about his true thoughts.

Zeb rubbed a hand down his face in frustration. He steered Jasper away from the people he'd been talking to, and headed down the street toward Curtis and a group of six other men, all fifty or older, who seemed as riled up as him.

The men's agitation settled somewhat as Zeb came to a stop among them.

"Here ta join us, marshal?" asked Curtis.

"Well now, that depends." Zeb glanced over the group. "What kinda evidence did you boys find ta think the Natives did this?"

"They're savages!" Curtis spat to the side. "What reason do they need?"

Zeb raised a hand at him. "Ain't what I asked you. We can worry about the why of it after we know for sure the who of it."

The men stared at him.

"Well, o'course they done it," blurted Curtis. "Who else would?"

"When's the last time anyone saw a Native around here?" asked Zeb.

"Couple weeks back," said a man with a long black beard sporting a few threads of grey. "Just ridin' around out there near the canyon."

"Plannin' an attack no doubt." Curtis spat again.

"How likely you reckon there'd be several weeks between a scout and an attack?" Zeb raised an eyebrow.

Curtis grumbled, cheeks reddening.

"Are you planning to simply ride back and forth across the desert hoping to find Natives to shoot?" asked Zeb.

"They ain't that far from here," snapped Curtis. "I know where to find 'em. Sure as I'm lookin' at you now, they took little Ada back there for whatever savage thing they mean to do."

"And where is that?" Zeb tilted his head.

"Southwest from here." Curtis stabbed a finger off to the side. "Everyone thinks they're in the canyon, but they ain't. In the woods, there's a crick split by a dead tree. Follow the water on the left. Couple hours, you'll be in their land. Got a village down there still. We ought not waste no more time. That poor, innocent girl's prob'ly already gone, but we can get revenge for her."

The men began to mumble amongst each other about Curtis having a point, and they'd tolerated the savages being close for too long.

Zeb gestured at the church building not too far from them. "You forgettin' the bit about 'thou shalt not kill?'"

"Tell them that!" Curtis scowled. "They come over here and kill ours. Godless heathens don't respect nothin'."

Zeb leaned back. "How do you know they did it?"

"Uhh." Curtis shot him a look as if to call him a moron. "Who else would?"

"Oh, any drunken outlaw wandering the desert might've come on by." Zeb pointed up. "The almighty created Heaven and Earth and everything on it, right?"

The men all nodded.

"That means he created the Natives, too." Zeb pointed at the church. "How ya reckon' he'd take to someone destroyin' his creations?"

Curtis stared into nowhere, seemingly confused. The other men waited for him to come up with an answer. By the expression on the man's face, Zeb figured he didn't much care what the Almighty had to say, he merely wanted an excuse to go shoot Natives.

Before the mental stalemate in Curtis's head came to

an end, Zeb slapped himself on the leg. "Well, I'd suggest you boys do somethin' more useful than standin' around here gettin' yourselves all worked up over figments of your imagination. If you men got enough vigor left in ya to go attack a Native village, you got enough in ya to go help look for the child. You find any kind o' proof o' who did it, I'll be right there with ya. But, ta go runnin' off and shootin' anyone ya think *might* be involved... well, that right there'll turn you into the same kinda savages you think they are... and land you in jail for murder."

With the men staring at him in stunned silence, Zeb clicked and nudged Jasper off in the direction of the juniper forest between downtown and the Lamb Ranch.

A heavy storm of irritation and guilt shadowed him as he entered the woods. The intermittent hoot of an owl carried through the trees, but otherwise, the forest held an almost unnatural stillness. While it didn't unnerve him, the placidity it had before no longer existed. He didn't waste time searching around for any sign of the creature. Even if he were to find it, the end result of another confrontation wouldn't be different than the first. He'd only accomplish losing eight to ten hours waiting to return from the land of the dead.

He *had* to go find Wind Hawk—which he assumed to be a person's name—to have any chance at confronting the revenant. Before he could do that, however, he needed to know what happened to Ada Lamb.

The Lady, or whatever master she served, chose him for the task of putting abominations down. Being charged with such a duty ostensibly ranked higher than any concerns of mortal law. If he had, in fact, taken the wrong path at the proverbial fork, he hoped with all the desire he could muster the small, fearless sprite of a girl

he'd last seen laughing and running around hadn't
suffered for his choice.

Chapter Twenty-four
Whisper

When Zeb emerged from the forest, he had a clear view across a mile or so of open land to the ranch house.

The sky was in a strange mood. Clouds directly overhead made the landscape dark, as if a storm threatened to roll in at any second. However, the distant canyon walls practically glowed from sunlight, the pale beige rock so bright he had to squint. The panorama in front of him seemed the product of a mad artist who didn't understand how light worked.

It quite likely meant nothing more menacing than an unusually dense—and large—cloud. With all the talk of revenants, Native curses, and relocated graveyards, not to mention Edmund Cartwright's untimely death in the same house the Lamb family now occupied… the surreal quality of his surroundings inherited a deeper sense of foreboding.

He gazed up at the thick grey mass. The enormous cloud hung over the property like a physical manifestation of worry and misfortune. A small group of people stood near the front of the main house. Zeb nudged Jasper up to a trot.

Isabelle Lamb alternatively paced about and leaned on an older woman to avoid collapsing. A hint of resemblance suggested it might be her mother. Two other women, both of whom looked too old to go traipsing about with a search party, hovered close, attempting to offer emotional support.

The four women fell silent at his approach, peering up at him on horseback. Isabelle's eyes widened as dread began to take over her expression.

Zeb raised a hand. "I ain't here to bring ya bad news, ma'am. Just to help out. I hear the little one's gone missing."

"Yes." Isabelle swallowed, exhaled, then looked down. "She wasn't in her bed this morning. No one saw her. They found Conrad and Leonard dead. Ada wakes up at every little thing. I'm terrified she might've seen it happen and whoever killed those men noticed her watching."

He tightened his jaw. His fears matched hers, only the nature of the killer differed. She assumed an ordinary man responsible. Zeb knew otherwise.

"Still lookin' for that bank robber?" asked the oldest of the women who appeared upward of seventy.

"Not anymore. He's in jail now. I'm here to help as best I can."

Isabelle pointed west. "Calvin and the others are spread out, searching for her. She ain't answering anyone calling for her."

"Pardon my directness, Mrs. Lamb, but where'd they find the deceased?"

"Over by the second house. You'd need to ask Calvin exactly where." She pressed a hand to her forehead. "I didn't see them."

"Couple steps from the outhouse," said the woman who appeared to be Isabelle's mother. "Reckon one went ta use it in the dark. T'other heard the ruckus o' him bein' attacked and got caught up in it."

Zeb nodded at her in thanks, then glanced to the right at the house the ranch hands used. The distance between the two buildings made it unlikely but not impossible for Ada to have heard or seen the killing.

"Anyone else not turn up?" asked Zeb.

"No, sir." Isabelle dabbed a tear. "Everyone able to is out there looking for her."

Crazily enough, the notion the undead monster might have simply befriended her and they walked off together made more sense than, say, one of the ranch hands being a depraved killer of children.

Zeb assured Isabelle he wouldn't rest until they found Ada before jumping down from the horse and heading around to the rear of the house to begin his search. Plenty of people already swept the countryside, so he figured it best to start by looking for any evidence of what might have occurred. The door did not appear to have been broken open, nor did he see signs of damage to the porch, the railing, or the walls—as if a creature like the revenant climbed to a second floor window. He spotted numerous footprints here and there of a size likely to be Ada's, though they may well have been days old. His dread of spotting an unusually heavy, plodding man's tracks beside the girl's did not come to fruition.

What the devil is going on?

A defeated sigh slid across the back of his mind. Not being able to tell much of anything from the tracks made him think of the ridiculously unrealistic Native American character in the novels he'd read as a teen. In the stories, that man could look at a patch of ground and somehow determine the entire outfit a person had been wearing when they walked there. To this day, Zeb still didn't know for sure if the author truly believed the Natives possessed such fantastical powers—or deliberately mocked them.

Isabelle's emotional voice carried over the house from the other side. She appeared to be rambling about how she'd never be able to cope with the loss of her youngest at such an age. Zeb bowed his head and closed his eyes, vowing to stay here until Ada turned up... and hoping he wouldn't find a body.

"Attic," whispered a voice as though a woman stood behind him on the left.

Normally, having a person come out of nowhere close enough to kiss would've made him jump. Mysteriously, this voice didn't startle him. More, it seemed a normal sort of thing one might have happen all the time.

He glanced back fully expecting to see no one there. Sure enough, he stood alone behind the house. That the disembodied utterance *still* felt as ordinary as anything bothered him more than it happening.

His thoughts turned to The Lady. He couldn't definitely claim to recognize a mere whisper of a voice. However, his matter-of-fact reaction to such an event implied familiarity. Either he imagined it or knew exactly who said it.

"Attic," muttered Zeb before peering up at the relatively small part of the building attempting to be a fourth story.

Edmund Cartwright certainly had grand plans. Who starts a ranch for the first time by building a three-story home? It fed into Zeb's opinion that people with too much money often did foolish things with it.

Nothing looked amiss with the house from here, so Zeb headed back around to the front where Isabelle and the older women now sat in the shade of the porch. Mae, the fourteen-year-old daughter, poured water for everyone. She paused to glance over at Zeb walking up the steps. The girl's reddened eyes said she'd spent most of the day thus far in tears.

He tried to reassure her with an 'everything will be all right' smile—to minimal effect.

"Did you find something?" asked the grandmother. "You look like a cat that got the canary."

Zeb removed his hat. "Ma'am. Last time I was here, I spoke to Ada and she told me she saw some manner of monster."

Mae covered her mouth, starting to cry again. Isabelle stared at Zeb, her expression shifting from worried sadness to a mixture of horror and hope. The three older women all rolled their eyes at the mention of the child's tales of monsters.

"She also told me she wakes up easy." Zeb shifted his gaze upward for a second. "I have to ask in the interest of being thorough, how well has anyone looked around the home, inside? Any chance she thought she saw the monster again, got spooked, and took to hiding? Perhaps, maybe, in the attic?"

The older daughter ceased weeping in an instant. She practically dropped the ewer of water in her mother's lap before darting into the house. Isabelle hastily shoved the pitcher into her mother's grasp, then scrambled out of the big porch chair to run inside.

Grandmother made a face at Zeb as if to say she now fully expected the girl's 'disappearance' to be nothing more than a misunderstanding. She also gave off a sense of 'how can my family be so dumb' while conveniently ignoring that she, too, had been of a mind something dire happened.

The other two women, likely friends of the grand-mother, clasped their hands and stared urgently at nothing in particular, the clear hope good news was imminent shone from their eyes.

An unintelligible woman's voice came from the house a moment later. It had to be Isabelle shouting, but whether it had been a word or merely a gasp of raw emotion, he couldn't tell. Soon after, the woman emerged out onto the porch carrying a disoriented and sleepy looking Ada, still in her nightgown. Mae trailed close behind, holding her younger sister's hand and giggle-crying.

Ada, blonde hair in an unruly frizz, gazed around at everyone with a baffled expression. The sight of her alive—and so unaware of the chaos she'd inadvertently caused—instantly brightened the lawman's mood and got him laughing. Grandmother set the ewer on the nearby tiny table, stood, and fussed over the child, muttering about how dirty she'd gotten from attic dust.

"How…" Whispered Isabelle. She stared at Zeb, clearly shocked at him knowing exactly where to look. "Never mind… it doesn't matter how." She squeezed Ada.

The girl peered at Mae, then her mother, then grandma, and finally Zeb. "Why are they all crying?"

"You gave your family a scare." Zeb patted her on the head. "They couldn't find you."

"I'm sorry." Ada yawned. "I didn't hear them calling for me. I's sleepin'."

"How'd ya not year 'em all?" asked Mae. "You wake when birds fly over the house."

Isabelle gave a teary laugh and squeezed Ada.

"I wasn't tryin' to sleep, but I sleeped anyway." Ada stifled another yawn.

"Poor thing likely tried to stay awake all night and passed out, exhausted," said Zeb. "You see something scary, hon?"

Ada nodded, then whispered, "The monster hit Mr. Gilliam an' broke his head like a egg."

The women all gasped.

"Like an egg?" asked Mae, horrified.

"Yes." Ada looked down. "It was dark. I didn't see much. Made the same noise like when Mama dropped a egg on the floor. Monster knew I's watchin' 'im. Looked right at me. I know 'cause his eyes are like candles. I ran off ta hide. Tried ta stay 'wake, but I sleeped behind Grandma's trunk." She peered at her mother. "Am I in troubles?"

"Of course not, sweetie." Isabelle squeezed her.

Zeb backed down the porch steps. "I'll go round up the others, let 'em know she's been found."

Chapter Twenty-five
Much About Fair

Two hours later, Zeb joined the family, a dozen ranch hands, and three older women for dinner.

No one seemed to care that very little work got done that day. Between the joy of finding Ada in good health and the disturbing somberness of two ranch hands being killed the night before, not even Calvin Lamb had any ability to think about work beyond the most necessary things like feeding the animals.

Meanwhile, Zeb assumed Ada had seen a bit more than she let on. This time, the small nine-year-old didn't act as if she'd merely discovered a dead cow out in the pasture. She kept still and mostly quiet, obviously frightened though not to the point of shivering or hiding under the table. Had he been a gambling man, he'd have wagered the girl would look for a hiding place as soon as it got dark.

Having seen what he'd seen... he didn't blame her one bit.

Once dinner ended, Zeb asked Calvin Lamb and his

oldest son, Everett, to step out onto the porch for a private conversation.

"What's this about now?" asked Calvin. "All evening you've been lookin' about like you expect to see that monster my daughter's dreamed up."

Everett stifled a chuckle.

Zeb smiled. "In all seriousness, I've seen a few things that have led me to keep a more open mind. While I can't say for certain what it is Ada saw last night, I believe she definitely saw something. Maybe a some*one*."

Calvin and Everett exchanged a glance.

"Obviously, someone attacked poor Leonard Coor and Conrad Gilliam, right?" asked Zeb.

The men nodded.

"I'm sure your daughter saw the person… or critter responsible." Zeb glanced from Calvin to Everett and back. "Now, she said the supposed monster's eyes glowed like candles."

"Could be moonlight reflectin' in the eyes." Calvin pursed his lips.

"But it ain't like Ada to make up stories of scary things. I mean, not until recently." Everett sucked a bit of dinner out of his teeth. "I think she did see *something*. No tellin' what though."

Calvin shook his head almost imperceptibly. "You're too grown for them kinds o' stories, Ev."

"Ain't a story, Pa. Even if she only saw a man, someone's been killin' our people." Everett flailed his arms. "We didn't imagine Ollie, Conrad, and Leonard dyin' did we?"

"What's your point, marshal?" asked Calvin.

"I'm goin' to be as straight with you as I can be, even if this might sound a bit crazy."

Calvin raised one eyebrow. Everett raised both.

"Seems a feller named Morris Poole might've got hisself cursed. Reckon he's come lookin' for revenge, curse and all."

"A native curse?" asked Calvin.

"Ayuh. Now, the stories I've been hearing about Morris don't sound like the sort of thing what might get a dead man comin' back to settle a score. Minor stuff. Wage disputes. What am I missing?"

Calvin shrugged. "Yeah, I remember him. The man made quite the fuss over six dollars." Calvin scratched his eyebrow. "He'd got it in his head we'd agreed on a wage of $18.50 a month. Now, that's not a bad wage for a ranch what doesn't give board. But the people who work for me eat and sleep fer nothin'. My rate's $16.50 a month, and I had the signed document—with his signature on it—as proof. After three months, he expected $55.50. When I gave him $49.50, he lost his composure. Lost it more when I showed him the work document."

"Man's prob'ly illiterate, Pa," said Everett.

"Can read numbers at least." Calvin glanced at the marshal's badge before making eye contact again. "I got all the ledgers and contracts if any judge needs ta see them."

"I highly doubt this matter will ever go before a judge. Sure as anything, you're going to think I've lost my mind, but I do believe it's Morris Poole responsible for the killings around here. It is also more than likely he ain't quite Morris Poole no more."

"Not following you." Calvin hooked his thumbs in his belt. "It's Poole but not him?"

Zeb took a deep breath. "You know all them stories about the canyon; in particular, that cave full of Native artifacts?"

Both men nodded.

"Well, seems ol' Morris found his way in there, broke something, and got hisself cursed." Zeb glanced off to the distant canyon. "Whatever the curse did to him, it's made him all sorts of ornery over that wage he thinks you owe him. Except what he's become don't care about money, or fairness."

Calvin bowed his head, chuckling at the porch. "You're right, marshal. That does sound crazy."

"Sure as anything, it does." Zeb fidgeted his hat around his hand. "Look, it may be nothin' more than the man ate something he found growin' in the cave and it drove him insane. Or it might be somethin' mankind has no explanation for. Whatever happened to Morris Poole, he's determined to cause hell for you and yours. I suggest you keep everyone inside after dark. If you spot him on your land at night, don't try to confront him."

"Why the hell not?" Calvin stood taller, indignant. "You're saying the man's killing my workers and threatening my family and you expect me *not* to run him off or shoot him?"

Zeb looked him in the eye. "I do. You're going to ask me why, to which I will ask you if you saw the bodies of the men he killed."

"I did," said Calvin in a somber voice.

"Skulls crushed?"

Calvin sighed. "Crushed kinda falls short of the totality of it, but I suppose it's a good a word as any."

Zeb pursed his lips. "Mister, he did that with his fist. Likely hit 'em just once. This thing ain't no man, to be honest with ya. I ran into him the night I hunted that bank robber. Your daughter isn't makin' up stories. But you don't have to take my word for it. If you see him, you'll know. It ain't no reflected moonlight. The poor bastard's eyes are lit up bright as fire light."

Everett shivered.

"Well, marshal." Calvin let out a long breath. "I've dealt with a lot of men over my years. A lot of men who'd try to take my last dollar if I let them. Lot of men lookin' to sell me things that ain't what they claim. Figure by now I've got a decent sense when a feller's lyin' to me. You said all that mess starin' me straight in the eye and didn't even blink. So, either you speak the truth or you've gone off the reservation, so to speak."

"He don' look crazy, Pa."

"No. He don't." Calvin pursed his lips, some of the color draining from his face. "Assumin' you aren't nuts, what can we do about it?"

Zeb put his hat on. "Keep your people inside at night. If you end up trippin' over the thing, try to light it on fire. God willing, you won't see it at all before I get back."

"Where are you going?" Everett stepped closer. "It's almost dark. Didn't you say not to go out at night?"

"I did." Zeb stepped toward Jasper. "This Poole feller ain't got no business with me. Hopin' he won't pay me no mind until I find out what needs to be done to be rid of him."

Calvin gestured east. "He had no business with the poor bastard they found on the road either."

"Aye, true." Zeb patted Jasper on the neck. "I saw the bastard once and walked away. Hoping I can do it again. The Natives beat the evil before. Hopin' they can help me beat it again."

"The Navajo did this?" asked Calvin, his voice and eyebrows rising.

"No. They fought some great ancient evil here many, many years ago and—according to legend—

sealed it up in the cave Poole disturbed." Zeb set to brushing Jasper. "Maybe they can tell me how to put it back."

"You be careful." Calvin offered a hand. "Thank ya kindly for your help finding Ada."

"Just glad it worked out to be nothin' bad." Zeb shook his hand.

"Aye. You be careful now," said Calvin. "No tellin' what to expect from the Indians if you go riding into their land. Ain't the most of friendly with us."

Zeb chuckled to himself. No great surprise, bad blood lingered on both sides. He couldn't say for sure who did wrong first, but the sort of pointless, blind hostility that men like Curtis Small clung to didn't help matters.

"What do we tell people?" asked Everett. "They ain't gonna much believe in the kinds of things you're talking about."

"Tell 'em I'm investigating the murders and there's still a killer out there." Zeb climbed into Jasper's saddle. "And for God's sake, stay inside after dark."

The men nodded.

Zeb nudged his horse into motion and rode off to the southwest.

Chapter Twenty-six
Wind Hawk

Starting a ride to a Native village right around sunset had to count among the most foolish things Zeb had ever done.

Around age ten, he almost burned down his grandfather's barn trying to prove his belief the story about magnifying glasses and sunlight was a lie. Turned out, the old man hadn't been teasing him. In hindsight, a barn full of dry hay did not make for the best place to conduct such an experiment. Fortunately, he'd been too frightened by the sight of fire to run away and lie about what happened and scrambled to tell his grandfather immediately.

They'd saved the barn… his backside, not so much.

I deserved that paddling.

Zeb chuckled under his breath.

He again rode into the juniper woods, pondering how to react if he encountered the revenant. As much as he disliked having to admit it, he didn't think a meeting with it could end in any way other than him dead again.

If he ran into it tonight, the best thing he could do would be to flee... unless he happened to have a ready source of fire nearby... or a damn sword. Hopefully, it wouldn't be able to find him if he remained quiet. Last time, it most likely heard the gunfire of two fools trying to kill each other.

Then again, it followed him the first night when he hadn't made a noise. And Zeb doubted either of the two dead ranch hands had made much of a ruckus going to the outhouse at night. Same with the traveler they found on the road. No one knew who he was or why he had been traveling to Harlon's Pass. Most likely, he was a simple cowboy or perhaps even an outlaw... but Zeb couldn't say for sure. Since he hadn't seen the man's corpse, he had no idea if his face matched any wanted notices.

Poor sumbitch might not even have a face anymore.

Zeb had a mind to believe the revenant could somehow sense movement. Maybe it tied in somehow with the curse. Hard to say one way or another.

Once Zeb started yawning, he decided to rest for the night. He didn't actually stop for another twenty minutes or thereabout until he stumbled upon a creek. While Jasper drank, Zeb ate his fill of hard tack then broke out a bedroll. Not wanting to waste the time building or cleaning up after a fire, he contented himself not to.

After settling down in as comfortable a position as a thin blanket over raw earth could be, he closed his eyes and let himself relax, intent on a deep sleep. Most would consider it unwise for him to lower his guard while sleeping alone in the middle of the forest, but being ambushed in the night would only make him sleep a few hours more...

...and he figured he could use the rest.

***

He followed the creek to the west after waking the following morning.

Nothing hurt nor had any items gone missing from his person, a good sign no one killed him in his sleep. Around about two hours after sunrise, he reached a spot where the creek forked around a large mound of dirt with a tree growing out of it. Curtis said 'the left water' led toward the Navajo territory. Depending on how one stood at the three-way intersection, 'left' could mean any of them. However, despite Curtis being a simpleton, it didn't take but a second for Zeb to decide which spur of the creek to follow.

One arm went back to the east, the way he'd come from. The other two went northwest and southwest. Since he knew the Navajo village was to the southwest, it made the choice of which creek to follow simple. Unfortunately, he didn't know too much about Natives beyond rumor and a few fiction novels that tended to either romanticize or demonize them.

Prior to his observing the raw savagery men could visit on each other during the Civil War, he might have been inclined to share the opinions of men like Curtis, believing his people to be somehow superior intellectually and spiritually. Any illusions to that effect died hundreds of times all around him while he watched brother tearing the guts out of brother, sometimes with their bare hands or pocket knives. Men who'd ordinarily have shared pleasant conversation over whiskey shot each other. When they ran out of powder or balls, they bashed each other's brains in with their empty muskets or used bayonets.

Zeb did not think it possible to truly hate a man you'd never met before... but the ghosts of the battlefield proved him wrong. Men he'd spent months marching, camping, sleeping, and fighting beside—men he *thought* he knew and understood—had displayed shocking brutality as bad or worse than any rumor claimed of the Natives. Being humans as well, he certainly accepted the Natives, too, had an equally apt chance of being murderous and violent as anyone else. But, like the supposedly civilized white men who comprised the armies of the North and South, they also had to possess a reasonable side.

Men were not violent monsters *all* the time, no matter where they came from.

He followed the creek while keeping a wary eye out for signs the revenant might attack. Though it seemed unlikely to be a problem during the day, he did not know for sure. The water varied in places, from a mere trickle to almost six feet across and at least knee deep. At approximately noon, he left the woods for open scrubland that stretched as far off as he could see to the horizon, dotted here and there with rocky hills. Zeb kept going for at least another two hours without stopping.

Not long after the hunger of his ignored midday meal grew strong enough for him to consider stopping to rummage food from his saddlebag, he spotted signs of civilization in the distance. A mixture of teepees, wooden shacks, and larger tents sat a modest walk's distance from the creek a bit more than a mile ahead.

The settlement looked suspiciously abandoned until the reason for its emptiness made itself known: two men watched him from behind a boulder a short distance from the facing side of the village. Both held rifles at the ready but not aimed at him. No doubt the men spotted him before he noticed the village and raised a warning, sending everyone else scrambling to avoid catching stray bullets.

Zeb stopped at what he believed to be a non-threatening distance and raised one hand in greeting.

The two Natives watching him glanced at each other briefly before staring at him for another minute or two. Finally, one of them jogged off toward the village and ducked into one of the larger, more elaborate shacks that came close to counting as a proper structure. Zeb remained where he stopped, Jasper taking the opportunity to nibble on something. The remaining man stood so motionless, Zeb briefly wondered if he looked at a man or a statue.

Minutes later, the runner emerged from the shack with a second, somewhat older man who wore a vest of long, multicolored beads similar to the ones adorning Keekuk. He gazed at Zeb from afar for a moment, then said something briefly to the younger man before going back inside. The younger man jogged back to the first sentry. A moment later, both men stepped out from behind the boulder and began to walk toward Zeb. Their demeanor appeared wary, but clearly not hostile.

At this, Zeb decided to dismount as a show of respect in case they viewed being talked down to from horseback poorly.

Neither of the two long-haired men were older than their early twenties. Shirtless, in long hide pants and moccasins, they both had the sinewy, muscular physique of those who lived a hard, demanding life.

"I am Kosumi," said the one on the left in passable, if halting English. The muscles in his bare chest and arms remained taut, bracing to respond to any act of aggression. "Why are you here?"

His question caught Zeb slightly by surprise. He'd been expecting to be chased off, threatened, or at least told he shouldn't be here and to go away. Minutes earlier, the older man in the bead vest seemed to have had a strange, knowing quality to his expression. Could he have possibly sensed whatever The Lady had done to the lawman? It took a few seconds for him to collect his thoughts at the unexpectedly friendly greeting.

Reckon these folks'll believe me more'n most.

"I spoke to the spirit of Keekuk," said Zeb in a slow —and hopefully not patronizing—voice. "He told me to find Wind Hawk. Do you know where I can find him?"

Kosumi relaxed, all the tension in his arms fading. He said something in Navajo to the man beside him, who also lowered his guard, leaning closer in a curious manner as if to study this outsider who so brazenly approached their village.

"Wind Hawk is here. He knew a white man would seek him." Kosumi shifted his rifle around to hang on a strap over his shoulder. "You are He Who Strides Between Worlds. I will guide you to him."

Zeb didn't know what to say back to the man calling him by the same name he'd only heard from a spirit. He couldn't honestly dispute it; after all, if one regarded being dead as going to another world, the name the Navajo ghost gave him proved apt.

Kosumi led Zeb to the village. Other men, women, and children emerged from various hiding places among the teepees, shacks, and tents to observe the outsider up close. The small ones seemed curious. Older teens and adults remained wary and distrustful. A few spoke to Kosumi in harsh words, but upon hearing his response, relented. They still regarded Zeb with disapproval but none did more than stare. He assumed they wanted him to ask whatever questions he had and leave as soon as possible.

Up close, the building where the man he assumed to be Wind Hawk lived resembled a simpler version of a frontier house. Decorative small blankets, clay pots, beads, and other assorted items hung from the walls. Rather than a door, the building had a pair of thick animal hide flaps like a tent.

Kosumi pulled one aside and held it for Zeb, who stepped inside.

The interior consisted of one large dirt-floored room, most of the ground covered in brightly colored and patterned rugs around a central fire pit. Above, the angled roof guided any smoke to a hole where it could escape. Around the walls stood shelves, a bed, two tables, and a collection of seemingly random items including muskets, bull horns, drums, and even a few small barrels. Wind Hawk sat on the rugs close to the fire pit, which presently gave off a thin trail of smoke with no visible flames. The air smelled of plant matter, tobacco smoke, and hide.

Zeb nodded in greeting and waited for some clue as to what he should do.

The older man gestured at him while speaking in Navajo.

Kosumi stepped up next to Zeb. "Wind Hawk says you battle a dark spirit my people made war with many generations ago."

"Yeah." Zeb glanced back and forth between the two men. "When I spoke to Keekuk, he said something about that. Gotta seal it back away somehow. Fix whatever that fool broke."

Kosumi translated. Wind Hawk nodded twice during the conversation, smiled at Zeb, then spoke again before standing.

"He must make ready for you," said Kosumi.

"All right." Zeb eyed the rugs but since no one else presently sat, he remained on his feet.

Wind Hawk meandered around the small house, rummaging shelves, tables, and a trunk. He gathered a small leather pouch, some beads, thread, feathers, and various bits of plant material, animal bones, and other ground-up powdery substances Zeb didn't recognize. Once he'd collected everything, he resumed sitting by the small fire pit.

Kosumi started to tug at Zeb's arm as if to say they shouldn't be inside during whatever ceremony was about to occur, but stopped when Wind Hawk waved at him. The elder cast a handful of powder into the tinder, which promptly sparked into flames. Over the course of the next twenty minutes or so, the medicine man chanted over the smoke while assembling beads, feathers, and thread into something of a necklace or pendant around a small animal skull, perhaps that of a prairie dog or some other animal of similar size. Upon finishing the talisman, he packed it into the pouch, added more powders, herbs, and bones, then cinched it closed and held it out at arm's length in the smoke.

When he resumed chanting over the completed pouch, Kosumi and the other man bowed their heads in reverence. Sensing it rude not to do the same, Zeb obliged.

Eventually, Wind Hawk raised the pouch up high and examined it in the manner of a jeweler appraising a diamond. Apparently satisfied, he waved at Zeb, beckoning him over.

The lawman stepped close to the smoking fire pit.

Wind Hawk spoke a few lines, then held the pouch

up as if offering it to him.

"He gives you this talisman." Kosumi moved to stand next to Zeb again. "He says there is a spirit door. This door is broken and must be made whole. Mend it, and hang the talisman on it. Our ancestors will draw the dark spirit back through."

Zeb took the pouch. "Please tell him I appreciate the help."

Kosumi translated. Wind Hawk smiled, said a few things, then leaned back, smiling wider.

Chuckling, Kosumi faced Zeb. "He says you do this because you have no choice, but also thinks you would do it, anyway."

"Aye." Zeb nodded. "He ain't wrong." Weirdly, a mental image of what the door should look like appeared in his thoughts, perhaps a vision from The Lady: several ordinary seeming wooden logs bound together with leather cording. "Where can I find this cave?"

After Kosumi relayed the question, Wind Hawk spoke at length.

"North from here where the mountains make a canyon," said Kosumi. "Ride into the gap. You will find a small footpath on your left, marked by our ancestors."

The same cave that spooked the people of Harlon's Pass. Okay, now that makes sense.

Zeb closed his eyes and nodded. It hadn't been the mere presence of Native American trappings that unsettled everyone. Not that any of them would believe it, but they must have sensed the presence of the revenant there and blamed the Navajo for the darkness. Fortunately, the townspeople only reacted by wasting the effort of digging up and moving a bunch of graves. He thanked whatever powers that be the townspeople hadn't listened to Curtis Small and tried to make war with this village.

Zeb amused Kosumi by repeating the directions on how to find this spirit cave. Once he felt confident he could find the place, he bowed in gratitude. "Thank you for your help."

Wind Hawk bowed as well.

Zeb, Kosumi, and the other warrior left the tent and made their way across the village toward where Jasper nibbled on whatever greenery he could find.

"The dark spirit will come for us when it is finished with the white man's curse," said Kosumi.

"White man's curse?" asked Zeb. "All of us or just the damn fool what set it loose?"

"Just the fool and his curse." Kosumi gestured to the northeast. "Many days ago, Wind Hawk spoke of this spirit. The fool's anger directs it at other white men for now."

Zeb cringed inside when he realized what the man meant. Evidently, the enmity between Morris Poole and the Lambs kept the revenant focused on attacking them. Once that stopped, it would come here and attack every Navajo it could find seeking revenge for being shut up inside a cave. He had a feeling it would do far worse here than break fences, smash windows, or attack a handful of people. He couldn't explain why it had thus far only killed a few ranch hands who had nothing to do with the wage dispute... until it clicked.

Or at least, he made certain assumptions.

If the dark spirit the Navajo sealed away had a burning need for revenge there may very well be a conflict going on inside the creature. Morris—or what remained of him—wanted to get back at Calvin Lamb while the spirit wanted to go after Wind Hawk and his people. Maybe being pulled in two different directions served to distract the revenant from fully committing to either murderous course.

Zeb shrugged to himself. Nothing else made a lick of sense.

After bidding thanks and farewell to Kosumi and the other warrior, Zeb climbed up on Jasper's back and set out for the canyon.

Chapter Twenty-seven
Skinwalker

The sun created a most bizarre spectacle as it began its descent on the opposite side of the ridge.

Deepening twilight surrounded Zeb on all sides except for where it seemed as though a cleft of daylight split the shadow of the hills in front of him. The land appeared to be rising upward, closing as a great mouth to swallow the last traces of day. Above the canyon, the sky swirled with brilliant reds and oranges that diffused to the indigo-black surrounding it.

Venturing to the source of a 'great evil' at night sounded like a dumb idea. However, wasting time on luxuries like rest might result in more people being hurt. The revenant had not yet attacked anyone in the Lamb family directly, a fortunate circumstance he did not wish to tempt. The violence had evidently gotten worse—three men killed all in one night. Zeb worried the creature hurtled toward a breaking point.

Morris Poole no doubt retained some sense of himself despite having become such a fiend. As with

Zeb coming to terms with the supernatural world, it stood to reason Poole would, too. While Zeb didn't have another presence inside his mind driving him to do things, he figured eventually Morris and the dark spirit would grow accustomed to each other. When that happened, all hell would break loose.

Thoughts of people gossiping about 'the night the whole Lamb family got massacred' drove him on faster. Already, he predicted the outcome. The revenant would kill everyone there, then move on to the Navajo village and do the same. Where it would go after that, he couldn't say—but it would likely pursue anyone it believed had a connection to its imprisonment.

Daylight faded from the giant gap in the rocks as he rode onward. By the time he reached the start of a dirt trail leading into the rocks, it had become full dark. Not far from the stone wall on the left side of the canyon sat a small, abandoned campsite.

A heavy sense of foreboding hung over the area. Staring at a tiny one-man tent, a rock someone had moved to serve as a seat, and the remains of a small fire pit made him as uneasy as a man waiting to hear whether or not a judge would send him to the gallows. The ominousness only worsened when he looked at the canyon. Moonlight cast the pale rocks in an unnatural azure hue, too bright to seem real.

Fear gave Zeb a momentary pause… until the oddity of it struck him as ridiculous.

What's a man who can't stay dead got to be afraid of?

He sighed.

"Probably a whole heap o' things worse than gettin' dead."

A seconds' thought of what might happen if the

revenant got its hands on little Ada, or Mae, or their mother pushed aside his fear. He dismounted and approached the abandoned campsite. It appeared that whoever pitched the tent left in a hurry, as they made no effort to cover their fire pit or even take any of their belongings with them. Finding a camp in this state typically meant the person who slept there met an untimely end.

Though the fire had long since burned out, he still kicked dirt to cover it as it felt the proper thing to do. Among the various items in the tent, he discovered a leather knapsack tucked under some blankets. He crouched to pull it out, then opened it.

The bag contained two hip flasks, several shirts, a pair of pants, three pairs of socks, a loaded and primed pistol, a small collection of canned goods, some bread harder than a rock, and a leather billfold with the initials 'MP'. Zeb checked the billfold, discovering $38. He closed it without taking the money, and held it up to look at the dark brown letters stitched onto the flap.

"Morris Poole," whispered Zeb. "Explains why it looks like no one's been here for a couple of months."

He glanced back at the open land between here and Harlon's Pass. For everything to still be sitting here, especially the money, gun, and canned goods, spoke to the superstition of the locals or perhaps the energy in the area keeping random wanderers away. No one had come out here far enough to discover this camp. Since dead men didn't need things, Zeb decided to take the satchel. Later, when he had the benefit of daylight, he'd examine the canned goods to see if any of them remained in trustworthy condition.

The money, gun, and clothing, he'd hold onto until he determined if Poole had any kin. The billfold containing less money than what Lamb would have paid him gave Zeb the impression Poole took his pay, purchased some provisions, and left town in a hurry, most likely heading for parts farther west.

Zeb stood away from the tent, holding the satchel. He couldn't say for sure what happened in the cave, but it was obvious Morris never returned to this campsite. The idea that a pouch full of herbs, beads, and animal bones would somehow defeat a strong-as-an-ox creature his bullets didn't even annoy almost made Zeb laugh. It seemed ludicrous, but so too did the notion of a revenant —and of men coming back from the dead.

Jasper gave a mild shudder of nervousness as they started the ride into the canyon. Unable to shake the feeling that someone or something was sneaking up behind him, Zeb peered over his shoulder every few seconds. If anything did follow him, it must be a spirit as he could see nothing corporeal. Undeterred, he continued deeper into the ravine. Even though it hadn't helped much last time, he gripped the handle of his Colt. More dangers than a revenant might be lurking out here in the dark, and hopefully, they wouldn't all shrug off bullets as easily as deputy sheriff Jim Carberry brushed aside his wife's pestering.

Humorous memories of how she often needled at him provided a much needed relief in mood. She often got on him about finding a safer manner of employment, one where he'd be less likely to get shot. She hadn't appreciated Jim telling her 'this is the frontier, a man's just as likely to get shot selling horse feed as wearing a badge.' Sheriff Ervin managed to calm her by pointing out judges tended to come down much more harshly on those who killed lawmen, so Jim had *less* of a chance of being killed.

Diamonds Gang notwithstanding.

Zeb didn't know if he agreed with the rationale. After all, the death penalty—which should have given most men pause—did not seem to be as effective a deterrent as it should be. While harsher punishment for shooting lawmen did, on the surface, seem like it would protect them, lawmen tended to get into more situations where they'd be likely to get shot. He grumbled to himself, thinking of the woman's ghost he'd seen on the train to El Paso. The poor lady had been shot in the side of the head, probably walking along minding her own business outside the bank Arnold robbed when a shootout erupted.

She prob'ly never knew what happened. Didn't deserve that no more than what this Poole feller got.

Perhaps being a lawmen *did* offer a degree of protection. If a random innocent woman could end up dead with no warning, it didn't seem as if the west was terribly safe for anyone. Outlaws might sometimes decide to flee rather than shoot men wearing badges—again, except for the Diamonds Gang who actively hunted those who tried to maintain law.

Realizing they still might be a problem got Zeb grumbling to himself in the manner of a boy with an unpleasant chore he'd been trying to avoid. For a brief moment, he sympathized with Ervin, hoping the Diamonds stayed away from Silver Mesa so he wouldn't have to bother with them again.

Amid the unearthly blue glow of moonlight on the rocks, Zeb finally spotted what appeared to be a narrow footpath making its way up the mountain wall on the left. As best he could tell, he'd gone a little under a quarter of a mile into the canyon. The short, but steep path led up to an opening in the wall roughly as high off the ground as the second story of a building. Native markings decorated the rock wall for the entire length of the trail. A wooden post topped with a carved wooden mask stood beside the entrance to a cave at the top.

To him, the markings looked like primitive cave art, but they likely conveyed a specific meaning, similar to the yellow 'danger – explosives' signs often posted near mines.

"Danger, ancient evil," muttered Zeb. "Do not open."

Jasper nickered.

"Well, boy. You're not fittin' up that sad excuse for a footpath. Gotta ask ya to wait here."

The horse flicked an ear.

He patted the animal on the neck, dismounted, and made his way up the treacherously narrow trail. The opening in the rock face forced him to stoop to get through, being about two-thirds the height of a door. Ahead lay a small, plain cave tunnel swallowed by darkness. The top of the passage only came up to his shoulders. To go in, he'd have to stoop most of the way over.

"Zebadiah Clemens, sometimes, you are a fool." He sighed at himself.

After climbing back down to the horse to retrieve a lantern from his saddlebag and light it, he once again ascended the steep path. At the top, he held the lantern up, shining it into the cave. The passage led into the hillside in a more or less straight line with a slight downhill grade. More painted markings adorned the walls on both sides. Smooth stone gave the impression the cave had been carved out of the rock a great many centuries ago by water that had since gone elsewhere. The stone bore no marks from cutting tools, nor did any moss grow upon the dried-out surface.

Each breath tasted like dust seasoned with a hint of death. Though he couldn't explain exactly where the feeling came from, staring into this cave stirred dread within his mind. The way some experienced miners seemed to refuse to go underground hours before a mine collapse, this cave threw off an overwhelming sense of imminent doom.

A proper sane man would not continue past takin' one look at this. I don't speak a damn word o' Navajo and even I can read this. Says 'get the hell outta here.' He shook his head. *A man in his right mind would not go in there. Says a bunch about ol' Morris Poole.*

Grumbling to himself, Zeb crouched low and entered the confining cave.

Says a bunch about me, too.

Not far past the entrance, the cave expanded in height and width, allowing him to stand straight and still have about two feet of open space above his head. He walked about thirty paces before reaching a fork. For no particular reason, Zeb went to the left.

A sense of not being alone kept the hairs on the back of his neck upright. As much as he didn't savor the idea of a direct confrontation with the revenant, part of him hoped it was here rather than back at the Lamb Ranch harming the innocent.

Jaw clenched, Zeb advanced into the dark, lantern held up high in his left hand. Out of habit, he rested his right hand on the handle of the Colt at his hip. The notion shooting it wouldn't do a damn thing angered him, but anger took up too much space inside his head for any fear to get in, so it served a purpose.

The passage he'd gone into had no markings painted on the walls. He kept going for a little while, wondering if he chose the right direction. Before doubt made him turn around—a dead end did. This cave came to an abrupt halt at an empty and unremarkable spherical room that would've been perfect for a bear to sleep in had any such animals lived in the area.

As fast as the limited light and space allowed him to move, he backtracked to the fork and went the other way. Fourteen paces later, lantern glow fell upon another dead-end alcove where three tiny decaying wooden tables sat in a chamber about the size of a casket stood up on end. Scattered through it were numerous clay pots, spilled dirt, desiccated feathers and animal carcasses, as well as a collection of shiny semiprecious stones. All of it appeared to have been tossed about haphazardly. Despite the condition of it all, the items gave off an undeniably strong sense of power.

The formation of the cave by water struck him as impossible due to both spurs being dead ends… until he noticed a few holes in the ceiling of the chamber. Water must have come trickling down from somewhere up above and, over the course of many thousands of years, burrowed out the stone. If the place had any spiritual significance or simply happened to be a convenient pre-dug prison the Navajo used to hold the 'ancient evil,' he couldn't say.

Zeb lowered his gaze to the ground. On either side of the tunnel lay a collection of ancient, rickety boards. They appeared to have once been stood up in place as something of a barrier between the chamber and the cave… almost like a faucet capable of blocking the flow of whatever supernatural energy radiated from the pots and urns.

Morris appeared to have stumbled in here and, may-be seeing the shiny green rocks through the gaps in the wood, thought he'd discovered treasure. Unfortunately for him, he'd only unearthed a stash of worthless clay pots and some agates. If, as Zeb assumed, the spiritual energy flowed like liquid, being dammed up in here must have allowed it to gather a great deal of force, which likely burst outward the instant Morris broke the seal.

Perhaps Poole didn't have time to be disappointed.

Zeb crouched to examine the wreckage. Eight wooden slats of varying height to match the generally circular shape of the tunnel were bound together by ancient leather cording. Poole had sliced the cording connecting the fourth and fifth boards, effectively dividing the rickety 'door' in half. Scraps of petrified leather and fragmentary bones on the ground appeared to be the remains of a prior shaman's work. There was also a pouch similar to the one Wind Hawk gave him. No doubt, Poole smashed it in his efforts to get at the 'treasure' he thought lay in the dark.

In order to repair the barrier, Zeb would need to find a way to replace the bindings between the boards at four points along its height where Poole sliced. As a matter of habit, he didn't routinely carry a bunch of leather cording around. He did, however, have some rope in his saddlebags which would probably do the trick. With the same care one might reserve for museum relics, he lifted each set of four connected slats and propped them up in place, arranging the shorter boards on the outside edges, the two tallest in the middle.

The flimsy collection of wood and leather didn't seem like it would be capable of stopping anything. Whether the ominous energy flowing from the clay pots passed through the gaps between the boards or, like a ghost, straight through the wood, he couldn't say. One thing he did know—the barrier wouldn't work until he at least tied it together into a single piece and hung the medicine man's pouch as instructed.

Once again grumbling to himself, he made his way back outside to the horse to get the rope. Hopefully, it wouldn't matter what he used to repair the door. The machinery of the universe shouldn't care if he used animal hide cords or modern rope. If the manner of repair had been important, surely Wind Hawk would have said something.

"Hell," he muttered. "Maybe I could dynamite this cave shut, too."

Jasper gave a nervous murmur.

"I know, boy. I know." Zeb spent a moment rubbing his hand along the horse's neck. "Almost done."

After calming Jasper a bit, he headed back up the trail to the cave and made his way inside to the broken 'door.' After setting the lantern on the ground at an angle to give him some light to work in, he proceeded to wind the rope around the two middle boards.

He'd just about finished tying the first knot at the uppermost join when a heavy hand crashed down on his left shoulder. Dark orange light cast the shadow of a head and broad shoulders on the wood in front of him—neither his own.

Ah, hell. Seems I'm about to have a chat with a certain Lady.

Chapter Twenty-eight
A Hair Too Slow

Stuck at the end of a cave with the revenant right behind him, Zeb expected he had about a second left to live.

Resigned to his fate, Zeb let his arms fall slack at his sides and waited for the inevitable death blow. His right hand bumped his knife, setting off a spark of thought. While it only had a nine-inch blade, it came much closer to being a sword than his guns did. Acceptance of imminent death brought a sense of fearlessness. The lantern-cast shadow of the revenant on the wall appeared to fall for his apparent surrender, drawing back one arm to bash in his skull in no great hurry.

Zeb yanked his knife from its sheath and thrust it behind him at the creature's exposed chest, aiming by feel. A wet crunch reverberated in the cave as steel pierced bone. He twisted to find he'd sunk about three inches of knife into the center of the dead man's chest. The revenant's glowing orange eyes flared bright in shock and anger.

Not waiting to see what it did next, Zeb hammered his left hand against the butt of the handle, driving the knife to the hilt in the creature's heart. The revenant gave a heavy grunt as it swooned to one side, seemingly too weak to stand. On the way down, it lashed out with a wild, flailing swing, striking Zeb in the left arm with the force of a falling timber.

The hit flung him off his feet and sent him flying chest-first into the cave wall. Zeb didn't realize he'd heard a loud *crack* until after he crashed to the ground and his left arm refused to move. He landed on his right side, feet by the partially repaired door. Near blinding pain shot up into his shoulder. The revenant also lay on its side, wheezing, straining to get a grip on the knife handle protruding from its chest.

While the attack appeared to have had a far greater effect on the creature than bullets did, the thing would eventually pull the knife out and be back on its feet. Pain screamed across Zeb's mind, but not from his lips. He pushed up from the ground, wobbling to his feet just as the revenant righted itself, jerked the knife loose and tossed it aside.

Time seemed to come to a standstill as they stood there, Zeb staring into its hollow candle-fire eyes.

"You dun messed up, Morris," said Zeb. "Maybe there ain't much of you left in there, but listen up in case there is."

The revenant stepped closer, its expression blank.

"Ain't treasure here. Just some old evil thing the Natives shut away. You didn't mean ta let it out. It took over your mind. Kick it the hell out if you can."

For a brief moment, the creature appeared to hesitate in contemplation, as much as a corpse could convey any sense of emotion. Zeb didn't trust it, though he hoped.

Alas, it soon refocused its stare and lurched forward with a wild clobbering swing of its right arm. Having expected his attempt to reason with the monster to fail, he'd been ready for an attack. Zeb dropped low, letting the heaving fist fly over his head. Then grabbed his knife from the dirt, popped up, and slashed at the revenant's throat before plunging the blade in the chest a second time.

When the creature staggered away, clutching its wounds, Zeb decided to exercise discretion.

He ran like hell, broken arm and all.

In the blurry haze of a few seconds, he'd gone too far out of the lantern light to see anything, pushing onward in the dark by feeling the walls. Noise coming up behind him made it unnecessary to look back. He didn't particularly want to see the two glowing spots of orange light, for he knew they'd be much closer than he wanted them to be.

Mysteriously, the revenant ceased crashing along after him.

At first, Zeb didn't understand what made the monster stop... until he slammed into a stone wall.

He'd taken the wrong fork. Rather than making it outside—he'd found himself in another dead end.

"Ah, hell and tarnation." Zeb, now far more annoyed than afraid, whirled around. "You're damn sure not about to make this easy on me, are ya?"

Two spots of orange light hovered in the dark about ten paces away. The revenant appeared to understand it had cornered him. They briefly stared at each other like a strange pair of gunslingers about to throw down.

"Well, come on. Get it over with," said Zeb.

The revenant stalked toward him.

Zeb couldn't see a damn thing except for the glowing eyes. His broken left arm throbbed with a distracting amount of pain. In that second, he decided he had two choices: stand there and die or put his trust in the words of Wind Hawk and try a desperate move.

He opted for the second choice.

When the revenant came within lunging distance, Zeb hurled himself at it, thrusting his knife blind at where he hoped the fiend's heart would be. Two inhumanly strong hands grabbed his broken arm. Zeb's battle cry became a roar of agony, but served only to give him desperate strength as they tumbled to the ground together, Zeb on top of the flailing dead man.

The instant the creature's grip faltered, Zeb knew he'd landed a strike close enough to the heart to briefly stun the fiend. Summoning up reserves of willpower he didn't realize he possessed, Zeb pushed himself up using the knife as a handhold. The revenant screamed in rage, feebly clawing at him as he climbed over it.

Zeb crawled into a scramble back to his feet, rushing toward the distant lantern light. The fiend's gurgling receded into the dark behind him. Heartbeat pounding inside his head, left arm shrieking in hot flaming agony, he sprinted back to the chamber, heading for the glow of the lantern, which continued to illuminate the ancient wooden barrier. Unable to lift his injured arm away from his side, he used his teeth as a second hand to help him tie knots in the rope, binding the boards together. Every time he moved, a lightning bolt of pain shot up the bone inside his left arm, sending a cluster of brilliant spots dancing across his vision.

For the lowest cording, too near to the floor to bite, Zeb shifted his hip close and gripped the rope in his trembling left hand. He let out a cry of anguish, resisting the urge to collapse. Death would be a release, merely a nap so deep he'd not realize the passing time. He'd wake up whole, free of pain... but at what cost? Imagining little Ada screaming in terror as the revenant came for her, Zeb forced his left hand to close, holding the rope. He ignored the shuffling scrapes of the revenant removing the knife and making its way through the cave toward him. Zeb hastily wound the rope around the boards and pulled it tight into knots. Each second, each footfall coming up behind him might be all the time he had left to stop the murder of an entire family.

The shambling footsteps had to be right behind him. He pulled the final binding tight and hurriedly yanked Wind Hawk's pouch from his pocket. The instant he hung the pouch on the rickety barricade, two iron-fingered hands grabbed him.

Damn... too slow.

Chapter Twenty-nine
Curse

His knife lay somewhere off in the darkened cave.

His guns wouldn't help.

Zeb stared at the pouch dangling in front of him, and waited to see where he woke up. Would the revenant leave him here where he fell or might it drag him off somewhere? The ranch hands and one traveler had been left where they died, but they hadn't been right in front of the source of the creature's power.

A new, chilling thought stalled the breath in his throat. If he died here, might the dark spirit take him, too?

Seconds stretched on without a killing blow landing on his head.

He flicked his gaze from the pouch to the orange light cast on the wall by the burning eyes of the creature... the *fading* orange light. A heavy wheeze blew a dry breath across the back of his neck. The hands holding him lost strength and fell away. The *thump* of a body hitting the ground broke the awful silence.

Well now... Zeb eyed the pouch. *Guess you did something after all.*

Another wheeze came from behind him, developing into a cough.

Unsure what to expect, Zeb turned cautiously. The revenant lay on the ground, lost to shadows behind the lantern, which still shone on the barrier sealing off the chamber. No longer sensing a threat nearby, Zeb eased down to one knee, twisting to pick up the lantern in his right hand and point it at the body.

Blood dribbled from Morris Poole's mouth. His face had warmed from deathly white to an 'almost dead' shade of pale. He now looked like an ordinary man who'd been mortally stabbed or shot, seconds before expiring.

"Tell me that didn't really happen," choked Morris. "I killed people?"

Zeb exhaled. "Wish I could. People died, but, maybe it wasn't you that did it but somethin' what got inta your head."

Morris closed his eyes and coughed again. "The little girl..."

"She's fine."

"Couldn't... do it. I stopped it from hurting her." Morris choked on a mouthful of blood. "You shot me."

"I did." Zeb nodded once. "You broke my neck. Let's call it even."

"How aren't you dead?" wheezed Morris.

"Could ask you the same thing." Zeb shrugged his right shoulder. "Some things just ain't worth askin'. If we'd been meant to know, we'd know."

"I don't remember much."—Morris coughed —"Couldn't do nothin' but watch most times. Damn Natives... their skinwalker got me."

Zeb exhaled. "It ain't theirs. They shut it up in here. It got loose when ya broke the barrier holdin' it back."

With a final gurgle, Morris stared off into eternity.

"Hmm. Probably shouldn't leave you here… somethin' tells me that would be bad."

A gentle hand rested on Zeb's broken arm. In an instant, the pain faded from blinding to simply awful. He glanced over at the red-haired Lady, still wearing the same bizarre toga-like dress as before, looking as if she'd stepped out of an old painting.

"Was wonderin' if you had a hand in this… well, whatever he is."

She smiled. "Revenant is as good a name as any."

"Right. Guessin' that's different from a skinwalker?"

"Not entirely." The Lady peered back at the reconstructed barrier, seemed satisfied. "A skinwalker is a different name for the same being. To you, Morris Poole was a revenant. To the Navajo, a skinwalker. Legends are shaped by the people who record them."

Tingling exploded in Zeb's left hand. He balled his fingers into a fist, doing his best not to wince. "I don't think I'll ever understand this stuff."

She brushed at his cheek, still smiling. "It is not important for you to understand every detail. It is important for you to be a bulwark against the darkness."

Various weird sensations in his arm and hand faded to a dull ache. He'd likely have a hell of a bruise but the arm once again moved when he wanted it to. "Reckon that much, I can do." He looked over at her. "Think I need to relocate these remains?"

The Lady nodded.

"Right. As bent out o' shape as this man got over money he weren't even owed, guess he'd get ornery over an improper burial."

She gave him a 'you are more right than you know' look before fading away.

The cave appeared noticeably darker for her absence.

"All right, Morris. Don't get your knickers in a knot. I'll get you in a proper graveyard. If you got any kin ta take yer worldly possessions, I'll see to it they get 'em—assumin' they can be found. You just stay restin' is all."

With a grunt, Zeb hoisted the body up over his shoulder and headed for the cave exit.

Chapter Thirty
A Lovely Idea

Days later, Zeb stood on the station platform at Silver Mesa, watching the train pull away in a whorl of steam and noise.

It seemed all so strange how Calvin Lamb and his family put the strange events aside in their minds. After bringing Poole's remains—as well as the bones he'd found in the woods—back to Harlon's Pass for a proper burial in their cemetery, he'd pulled Calvin and Everett aside to give them as true an explanation of events as he felt they could handle. Even though he got the sense they believed him, the story they passed on to the family went something along the lines of an unknown crazy person who'd befriended Morris before killing him decided to stalk the family after learning of the bad blood over wages in hopes everyone would blame Morris.

As far as anyone would ever hear tell of, all the killings in Harlon's Pass were the work of an ordinary—albeit completely insane—man. It didn't matter to Zeb what anyone believed. Some lies served a good purpose when the truth sounded impossible. What difference would it make to insist on everyone accepting the real story?

He also suspected little Ada continued to believe a 'monster' did it.

The notion that 'monsters' might not all be completely consumed with darkness gave him pause. His task to deal with these sorts of things sounded an awful lot like it wouldn't be as simple as find and kill whatever caused problems. Perhaps he might've been able to save Morris Poole after all if he'd done something different. The more he thought of it, the more it seemed all the injuries the revenant sustained came back at once as soon as the curse broke. Zeb might not have been the first or only person to shoot, stab, or otherwise try to kill the fiend, but he certainly put several lethal bullets into the body.

Morris Poole had been every bit a victim as everyone the revenant smashed.

Did the best with what knowin' I had. No sense feelin' like I killed a man. He'd have been dead either way.

Zeb stood there in the blowing steam and smoke, watching the train roll off. Gradually, the bustle and chaos of the coal-fired locomotive faded, only to be replaced by the soft tapping of a woman's boots on the platform boards drawing nearer.

"Good morning, marshal," said Laura as she came to a stop beside him. "Are you seeing off friends or family?"

He smiled at her. "Neither. This is work related. Harry McDonald."

"Who?" She blinked.

"He's the second bank robber to walk away alive.

Just sent him east to El Paso."

"You aren't escorting him?"

"Don't need to this time. Couple o' marshals came to pick him up. Just as well. I need a bit of rest."

She tilted her head, giving him an appraising glance. "So you're not about to run off somewhere right away?"

"Not if I have anything to say about the matter." He winked.

"I see." She flashed a playful little smile. "Speaking of work… I've decided to take the rest of the day off."

Zeb politely kissed her, the sort of kiss respectable folks did in public. "Reckon I could use a breather as well."

Laura offered her arm. "Shall we go for a walk? The sky is lovely today… and I've got Morton to look after Heath for a bit."

"Why Ms. McCormick, that sounds like a lovely idea." Zeb took her arm. "I can think of nothing I'd enjoy more."

She smiled, a sparkle in her eyes.

Zeb walked with her off the train platform, heading wherever fate—and Laura—decided to take him.

The End

Zeb Clemens will return!

About J.R. Rain:

J.R. Rain is the international bestselling author of over seventy novels, including his popular Samantha Moon and Jim Knighthorse series. His books are published in five languages in twelve countries, and he has sold more than 3 million copies worldwide.

Please find him at: www.jrrain.com.

About Matthew S. Cox:

Originally from South Amboy NJ, **Matthew S. Cox** has been creating science fiction and fantasy worlds for most of his reasoning life. Since 1996, he has developed the "Divergent Fates" world, in which Division Zero, Virtual Immortality, The Awakened Series, The Harmony Paradox, and the Daughter of Mars series take place.

Matthew is an avid gamer, a recovered WoW addict, Gamemaster for two custom systems, and a fan of anime, British humour, and intellectual science fiction that questions the nature of reality, life, and what happens after it.

He is also fond of cats.

Please find him at: www.matthewcoxbooks.com

Made in the USA
Middletown, DE
13 November 2024

64491272R00124